SECOND FORM AT
MALORY TOWERS

Enid Blyton

SECOND FORM AT
MALORY TOWERS

DEAN

First published in Great Britain 1948
Reissued 2009 by Dean
an imprint of Egmont Books Limited
239 Kensington High Street, London W8 6SA

ENID BLYTON ® Copyright © 1948
Chorion Rights Limited.
All rights reserved.

ISBN 978 0 6035 6424 6

1 3 5 7 9 10 8 6 4 2

Printed and bound in Singapore

Contents

1 Back to Malory Towers again

'I've simply loved the hols,' said Darrell, as she got into her father's car, ready to set off to school once more. 'But I'm glad it's time for school again. I've been eight weeks away from it!'

'Well, well, how simply terrible!' said her father. 'Is your mother ready, or must I hoot? It's an extraordinary thing that I'm always the first one ready. Ah, here comes Mother!'

Mrs. Rivers hurried down the steps. 'Oh dear, have I kept you waiting?' she said. 'The telephone went at the last minute. It was Sally Hope's mother, Darrell, asking what time we shall be along to pick up Sally and take her with us.'

Sally Hope was Darrell's best friend. Mr. Rivers, Darrell's father, was driving them both down to Malory Towers, their school in Cornwall. They were setting off very early so that they would be there before dark, and Sally was going with them.

'I hate leaving home but I just can't help being excited at going back again,' said Darrell. 'This will be my fifth term at Malory Towers, Mother – and I'm to be in the second form. I *shall* feel grand!'

'Well, you're thirteen now, so it's time you went up,' said her mother, settling down in the car. 'You will quite look down on the first form, won't you? – think they are mere babies!'

'I suppose I shall,' said Darrell, with a laugh. 'Well, the third form look down on *us* – so we're all kept in our places!'

'There's your little sister waving to you,' said her father, as the car slid down the drive. 'She will miss you, Darrell.'

Darrell waved frantically. 'Good-bye, Felicity!' she yelled. '*You'll* be coming to Malory Towers sometime, then we'll go together!'

The car purred out of the drive into the road. Darrell took a last look back at her home. She would not see it again for three months. She felt a little sad – but then, being a sensible girl, she cheered up at once and set her thoughts on Malory Towers. She had grown to love her school very much in the last year, and she was proud that she belonged to it. Four terms in the first form with Miss Potts lay behind her – now she had a year in the second form to look forward to.

They arrived at Sally Hope's house in an hour's time. Sally was ready for them, her school trunk and her nightcase standing beside her on the steps. With her was her mother, and by them stood a toddler of about eighteen months, clutching at Sally's hand.

'Hallo, Sally! Hallo, Daffy!' shouted Darrell, in excitement. 'Good, you're ready!'

The trunk was put in the boot at the back of the car, with Darrell's. The night-case was strapped on the grid. Sally's lacrosse stick was shoved in with the odds and ends, and then she got in herself.

'Want to come too!' called Daffy, her eyes full of tears as she saw her beloved Sally going away.

'Good-bye, Mother dear! I'll write as soon as I can!' called Sally. 'Good-bye, Daffy darling.'

The car slid off again, and Daffy began to howl. Sally looked a little upset. 'I hate leaving Mother,' she said, 'and now I hate leaving Daffy, too. She's lovely now – she can run everywhere, and she talks awfully well.'

'Do you remember how you hated her when she was a baby?' said Darrell. 'Now I bet you wouldn't be without her. It's fun to have a sister.'

'Yes, I was horrid to her,' said Sally, remembering. 'That was an awful first term I had at Malory Towers – I was so miserable, thinking I'd been sent away from home to make room for Daffy, the new baby. I hated you too, Darrell – isn't it funny to think of?'

'And now we're best friends,' said Darrell with a laugh. 'I say – who do you think will be head of the second form this term, Sally? Katherine's in the third form now, so she won't be. It'll be somebody else.'

'Alicia perhaps,' said Sally. 'She's about the oldest.'

'I know – but do you think she would make a good head?' said Darrell, doubtfully. 'I know she's awfully clever, and gets top marks in anything – but don't you think she's too fond of playing the fool?'

'She might stop that if she was head of the form,' said Sally. 'What Alicia wants is a bit of responsibility, *I* think. She just won't take any. You know she was asked to run the nature walks last term, and she wouldn't. But I can think of another reason why she wouldn't make a good head-girl.'

'What?' asked Darrell, enjoying this gossip about her school fellows.

'Well, she's rather hard,' said Sally. 'She wouldn't bother to help people if they were in trouble, she wouldn't bother herself to be kind, she'd just be head of the form and give orders, and see that they were kept, and nothing else – and you do want something else in a head-girl, don't you think so?'

'Well, who do you think is fit to be head of the form?' demanded Darrell. 'What about *you*? You size people up awfully well, and you're fine when anybody's upset or in trouble. And you're so – well, so *steady*, somehow. You don't fly off the handle like I do, or get all worked up about things. I'd love you to be head.'

'I wouldn't want to be,' said Sally, 'and, anyway, there's no chance of it. I think *you* would be fine as head of the form, Darrell – you really would. Everyone likes you and trusts you.'

For a wild moment Darrell wondered if it was possible that she might be chosen! It was true that all the girls, except one or two, really liked and trusted her.

'But there's my temper, still,' she said, regretfully. 'Look how I flared up last term when Marigold ticked me off at tennis, thinking I was somebody else. I didn't know she'd make a mistake, of course – but just think how I yelled at her and flung my racket down and stamped off. I can't think what came over me.'

'Oh, the sun was too much for you and lots of us that day,' said Sally, comfortingly. 'You don't usually lose your temper for silly things like that. You *are* learning to keep it for things it's useful for! Like going for that ass of a Gwendoline Mary, for instance!'

Darrell laughed. 'Yes, she really is an idiot, isn't she?

Do you remember how silly she was over Miss Terry, that singing mistress we had last term – the one that took Mr. Young's place for two months? I thought Miss Terry was stupid to put up with it.'

'Oh, Gwendoline will always be silly over *some*body,' said Sally. 'She's that kind. I expect she'll pick on somebody this term too, to worship and follow round. Well, thank goodness it's not likely to be *me*!'

'I hope there'll be some new girls,' said Darrell. 'It's fun sizing them up, isn't it? – and seeing what they're like.'

'There are sure to be some,' said Sally. 'I say – wouldn't it be funny if Mary-Lou was told to be head-girl!'

Both girls laughed. Mary-Lou was devoted to both Sally and Darrell, though Darrell was her heroine – and the girls liked little Mary-Lou very much. But she was such a timid little thing, shrinking away from all idea of responsibility, that it was quite funny to picture her face if she was ever told she was to be head of the form.

'She'd have a blue fit and go up in smoke,' said Darrell. 'But she's *much* better now, Sally. Do you remember how she used to shake at the knees when she was scared? She hardly ever does that now. We've all been decent to her and not scared her, and we've made her believe in herself – so she's different. She'll never be so bad again.'

It was a long, long drive to Cornwall. The journey was broken by picnic meals, taken by the wayside, sitting on heather or grass. Mrs. Rivers took the wheel of the car once to relieve her husband. The girls sat at the back and talked or drowsed, as the journey lengthened out.

'Not very far now,' said Mr. Rivers, who was back at the wheel. 'We may see some other cars on their way to the school, too. Look out for them.'

They soon saw one – a low red car belonging to Irene's people. Irene was at the back and waved violently, almost knocking off her father's glasses, as he sat at the wheel. The car swerved.

'Isn't that just like Irene,' said Sally, with a grin. 'Hey, Irene! Had good hols?'

The two cars kept more or less together, and the girls looked back at Irene's merry face. They liked her. She was a clever girl, especially at music, but a real scatter-brain otherwise, always forgetting things and losing them. But she was so good humoured that nobody could be cross with her for long.

'There's another car! Whose is it?' said Sally, as a third one came in from a side road, complete with school trunk at the back. It swung away ahead of them.

'One of the bigger girls,' said Darrell. 'Looks like Georgina Thomas. I wonder who will be head of the whole school this year. Pamela's gone now. I hope Georgina won't. She's too bossy for anything.'

Now they were very near the school and it suddenly came into sight round a corner. The girls looked at it in silence.

They both liked their school immensely and were very proud of it. They saw the great grey building, with a rounded tower at each end – North Tower, South Tower, East and West. A creeper, now turning red, climbed almost up to the roof.

'Our castle!' said Darrell, proudly. 'Malory Towers. Best school in the world.'

Soon the car swung up to the big flight of steps leading to the great front door. Other cars were in the drive, and groups of chattering girls stood about. Happy voices called across the drive.

'Hallo, Lucy! Look, there's Freda! Isn't she suntanned? Had good hols, Freda? You look as if you'd lived in the water, you're so tanned.'

'Hallo, Jenny! Did you get my letters? You never answered one, you pig. Hey, Tessie. Look out for my night-case. Take your great feet off it!'

'Good-bye, Mother! Good-bye, Daddy! I'll write as soon as I've settled in. Don't forget to feed my pet mice, will you?'

'Get out of the way there! You'll be run over by that car! Oh, it's Betty Hill. Betty, Betty! Have you brought any tricks or jokes back with you?'

A pair of wicked eyes looked out of the window of the car, and a tuft of hair fell over a brown forehead. 'I may have!' said Betty, stepping out. 'You never know! Anyone seen Alicia? Or hasn't she come yet?'

'The train-girls haven't arrived! The train is late, as usual!'

'Darrell! Darrell Rivers! Hallo, there! And Sally. I say, let's go in and find our dormy. Come on!'

What a noise! What a tumult! Darrell couldn't help feeling thrilled. It was good to be back at school again – back at Malory Towers.

2 Three new girls

Darrell said good-bye to her parents and they purred off in the car. Darrell was always glad that her father and mother were sensible when they said good-bye. They didn't burst into tears as Gwendoline's mother always did. They didn't expect her to stay close beside them and look mournful. They laughed and talked just as usual, promised to come down at half-term, then kissed her good-bye, and went, waving cheerfully.

Soon she and Sally were carrying their night-cases up the steps into the big hall. They had their lacrosse sticks too, which got entangled with people's legs as the other girls surged around and about.

Miss Potts was in the hall. She had been their form-mistress when they had been in the first form, and was still their house-mistress, for she was in charge of North Tower, in which they slept. All the girls' bedrooms or dormitories were in the four towers, and there was a house-mistress in charge of each one, and also a Matron.

Miss Potts saw Sally and Darrell and called them. 'Sally! Darrell! Take charge of this new girl for me, will you? She will be in the second form with you, and will be in your dormy. Take her up to Matron.'

Darrell saw a tall, thin girl standing by Miss Potts, looking nervous and scared. Darrell remembered how lost she had felt when she had first come to Malory Towers, and she felt sorry for the girl. She went up to her, Sally behind her.

'Hallo! Come along with us and we'll look after you. What's your name?'

'Ellen Wilson,' said the girl. She had a very pale face and looked tired out. In the middle of her forehead was a deep line, cutting down between her eyebrows, making her look as if she was continually frowning. Darrell didn't much like the look of her, but she smiled at Ellen kindly.

'I expect you feel pretty muddled with all this row going on,' she said. 'I felt the same last year when I came. My name's Darrell Rivers. And this is my friend, Sally Hope.'

The girl gave polite little smiles and then followed silently behind them. They all made their way through the excited throng of girls.

'There's Mary-Lou!' said Darrell. 'Hallo, Mary-Lou! You've grown!'

Little Mary-Lou smiled. 'I hope so!' she said. 'I'm tired of being the smallest in the form. Who's this?'

'Ellen Wilson. New girl. Second form,' said Darrell.

'In our dormy,' added Sally. 'We're taking her to Matron. Hallo, here's Irene. Irene, we saw you nearly knock off your father's glasses in the car, when you waved to us.'

Irene grinned. 'Yes, that was the third time I'd done it. He was just getting annoyed with me. Are you going to Matron? I'll come along too.'

'Got your health certificate?' asked Sally, slyly. It was a standing joke with the girls that Irene always arrived without it, no matter how safely her mother had packed it in her night-case, or given it in an envelope to Irene to put in her pocket.

'Got yours?' said Darrell to Ellen Wilson. 'We have to hand them over at once. And woe betide you if you go down with measles or chicken pox or something if you've just handed in a certificate saying you haven't been near anyone ill! Golly, Irene, you don't *really* mean to say you haven't got yours again?'

Irene was feeling in all her pockets, with a humorous look of dismay on her face. 'Can't find it at the moment,' she said. 'Must be in my night-case. But no – Mother said she wasn't going to put it in there anymore because it always disappeared. Blow!'

'Matron said she'd isolate you next time you came without a health certificate,' said Sally. 'You'll have to be in the san for two days till your mother sends another one. You really are an idiot, Irene.'

Feeling frantically in all her pockets, Irene followed Sally, Darrell and Ellen to North Tower, and went in with them. The second-form dormy was not far from the first-form dormy, where Darrell had slept for the last four terms. It was on the second floor and was a lovely big room with ten white beds in it, each covered with a pretty quilt.

The girls dumped their night-cases down in the dormy and went to look for Matron. Ah, there she was, shepherding another new girl up to the dormy. Darrell looked at the girl. She was about the same age as Darrell and, like Darrell, had black curly hair, but cut much shorter, more like a boy. She looked rather dirty and untidy, but she had a very attractive grin, and her eyes twinkled as she looked at the other girls. She did not look nearly so lost or forlorn as Ellen.

'Ah, Sally – Darrell – here's another new girl,' said Matron, briskly. 'Take charge of her, will you? Her name is Belinda Morris. Now – have you all got your night-cases? And what about your health certificates?'

'Our night-cases are there,' said Darrell, pointing to where they had dumped them on the floor. 'And here's my health certificate, Matron.'

'Where's *my* night-case?' said Belinda, suddenly.

'Surely you had it with you a minute ago?' said Matron, looking all round. 'Well, give me your certificate and then go and look for your case.'

'But it's in the case,' said Belinda, and looked vaguely round.

'You probably left it down in the hall for everyone to fall over,' said Matron. 'You girls! Thank you, Darrell. Is this your certificate, Sally? – and yours, Mary-Lou – and yours, Ellen. What about yours, Irene?'

'It's a most peculiar thing, Matron,' began Irene, hunting in all her pockets again. 'You know, I *had* it when I started off this morning. I remember Mother saying . . .'

Matron stared at Irene, really exasperated. 'Irene! Don't dare to tell me you've not brought it again. You know what I told you last term. There is a rule here that girls who forget their health certificates shall be isolated until one is produced. I've never had to enforce that rule yet – but in your case I really think . . .'

'Oh, Matron, don't isolate me!' begged Irene, taking her night-case, opening it and emptying all the contents higgledy-piggledy on the floor. 'I'll find it. I will!'

The girls stood by, laughing. Really, Irene was very funny when she had lost something. Matron looked on grimly. Irene bent low over the case, hunting hard – and suddenly she gave a cry and put her hand to her chest.

'Oooh! Something's pricking me! Whatever can it be? Gracious, something's run a sharp point right into me!'

She stood up, rubbing her chest. Then she opened the front of her coat – and the girls gave a scream of laughter.

'Irene! You donkey! You've got your health certificate pinned on to your front! You couldn't lose it if you wanted to.'

Irene looked down, pleased. 'Of course!' she said, unpinning it. 'I remember now. I *knew* I should lose it unless I really did hang on to it somehow – so I pinned it tightly to my front. Here it is, Matron. You won't have to isolate me after all!'

Matron took it, and put it with the others she had. 'A narrow squeak for you, Irene!' she said, and her plump face broke into a smile. 'You put a grey hair into my head at the beginning of every term! Now, you girls – unpack your night-cases and put out your things. The trunks won't be unpacked till tomorrow – and then each of you will have to check the clothes' list you brought with you.'

She departed, rustling in her apron, looking out for more returning girls, collecting lists and names and certificates, bringing order out of confusion, and welcoming back all the sixty or so girls returning to North Tower. In the other towers, three more Matrons were doing the same thing. It was a real task to welcome back about two hundred and fifty girls, with their trunks, nightcases and odds-and-ends!

Belinda had wandered off to look for her night-case. Whilst the others were still putting out their things, she sauntered back, a brown suitcase in her hand. She opened it and shook out a pair of pyjamas. She stared at them in surprise.

'Golly! I didn't know I had pyjamas like this,' she said. 'And what posh bedroom slippers Mother has put in for me. For a surprise, I suppose!'

Darrell looked over her shoulder. Then she grinned. 'You'll get into trouble if you unpack any more of those things,' she said. 'They belong to Georgina Thomas! She'll be jolly wild if she finds our you've got her night-case! She's probably hunting all over the place for it now. Can't you read, Belinda?'

Darrell pointed to the name marked on the collar of the pyjamas. 'Georgina Thomas'.

'Goodness, what an ass I am!' said Belinda, and stuffed all the things back untidily into the case. 'I thought it was *my* case!'

She went out of the room again, presumably to hunt once more for her lost case. Darrell grinned at Irene.

'I don't know what we're going to do if we have *two* people like you, Irene!' she said. 'One's bad enough – but *two*! You'll drive Mam'zelle cracked between you. And as for Miss Parker, our form-mistress – well, you know what she is! She can't stand anything vague or careless. We shall have some fun this term with you and Belinda in the class together!'

Irene didn't in the least mind being teased. She was a clever, good-humoured girl, brilliant at music, but very thoughtless and vague over the ordinary little everyday things. If anyone lost a grammar book it was Irene. If anyone forgot to turn up at a special lesson, it was Irene.

And now here was another girl, Belinda, who seemed to be just as bad. Irene very much liked the look of her, and had already made up her mind to be friends.

Belinda soon came back again, this time, fortunately, with her own case. She tipped everything out, and then proceeded to put her things in place, just as the others did – pyjamas under the pillow – tooth-brush, face-flannel, tooth-paste and sponge on a glass ledge at one end of the dormy, where the wash-basins were. Brush and comb in their bag inside the top drawer of the dressing-table. Then the empty night-case was put with the pile outside in the corridor, waiting to be taken to the box-room.

There came a great clatter up the stairs and the girls in the dormy raised their heads. 'The train-girls! They've come at last. Aren't they late!'

More girls clattered into the dormy. Alicia Johns came in, her eyes bright. Behind her came Jean, the straightforward, sensible Scots girl. Then came Emily, a quiet girl whose only real interest was sewing, and the most elaborate embroidery.

'One, two, three, four, five, six, seven, eight of us,' said Darrell, counting. 'Two more to come. Who are they?'

'Gwendoline Mary for one, I suppose,' said Irene, with a grimace. 'Dear Gwendoline Mary! I expect her mother is still sobbing over letting her darling lamb go away from her! Who's the tenth?'

'Here comes Gwendoline,' said Darrell, and the girls heard that familiar, rather whining voice. Gwendoline was a spoiled only child, and although Malory Towers had done her a lot of good, the holidays always seemed to make her worse again.

She came in – and with her was the tenth girl. Gwendoline Mary introduced her. 'Hallo, everyone! This is Daphne Millicent Turner, a new girl. She's in our form and in our dormy. She travelled down in my carriage and I'm sure she's going to be a favourite with all of us in no time!'

3   First day of term

This, of course, was a silly way to introduce any new girl, especially as every listening girl immediately felt that anyone likely to be Gwendoline's favourite was not at all likely to be theirs! They smiled politely at the new girl, taking her in from top to bottom.

She was very pretty. Her golden hair curled about her forehead, and her eyes were much bluer than Gwendoline's large pale ones, but they were set nearer together than Gwendoline's, giving her rather a sly look. She had beautiful white teeth, and a very charming smile.

She used it now. 'I'm so pleased to come to Malory Towers,' she said. 'I've never been to a school before.'

'That's one thing we had in common!' said Gwendoline, in a pleased voice. 'I didn't go to school before I came here either.'

'It would have been better for you if you had,' said Alicia. 'You wanted a lot of licking into shape,

Gwendoline. I suppose, as usual, you were waited on hand and foot at home these hols, with your old governess and your mother telling you that you were the most wonderful girl in the world!'

Gwendoline looked annoyed. 'You don't need to be rude immediately you see me, Alicia,' she said. 'Come along, Daphne, I'll show you what to do. You are in our dormy, which will be very nice. I can show you round quite a lot. I know how I felt when I first got here and didn't know anyone.'

Daphne seemed very grateful. She had very good manners, and thanked everyone nicely whenever they showed her or told her anything. She certainly was very pretty and graceful. It was clear that for some reason Gwendoline had quite made up her mind to be her friend and helper.

'I told you she'd have to be silly about *some*body,' said Sally to Darrell, as they went downstairs to their supper. 'Well, she's welcome to Daphne. She's got too many airs and graces for me!'

'Gwendoline says that Daphne's father is practically a millionaire,' said Darrell. 'She had a nanny *and* a governess before she came here!'

'Oh – so that's why dear Gwendoline is sucking up to her!' said Sally. 'I thought there must be *some*thing. Hey, Irene – you've still got your hat on! Do you particularly want to wear it at supper?'

'Oh, gosh!' said Irene, putting her hand up to her head. 'Have I forgotten to take it off? Belinda, you might have told me!'

Belinda grinned. 'I don't know that I noticed it,' she

16

said. 'So many things strike me as odd here, at the moment. Wearing a hat to supper didn't seem to be anything out of the ordinary.'

'What a pair you'll make!' said Sally. 'Come on, Darrell, come on, Mary-Lou. We shan't get any supper if we don't hurry.'

All the girls were tired that night, and the second-formers were very glad to tumble into bed. Gwendoline had chosen the bed next to Daphne. 'If you feel homesick, just tell me,' she said to Daphne, who looked really charming in blue pyjamas, her curly hair all about her shoulders in a golden mass. Gwendoline's hair, too, was golden, but it was straight. She envied Daphne her curls.

'I expect I shall feel rather strange,' said Daphne, getting into bed. 'You see, I'm so used to lots of people round me – Mummy coming to kiss me goodnight – and my governess popping in to see if I'm all right – and my nanny folding all my things. I shall . . .'

'No more talking,' said Sally, suddenly.

Gwendoline sat up. 'You're not head of form *or* dormy, Sally,' she said. 'Don't give orders, then!'

'I'm not,' said Sally. 'You know the rules, Gwendoline. I'm just reminding you of them, that's all.'

Gwendoline lay down. Presently the whispering began again. Sally got cross.

'Shut up, Gwendoline. It's long past time to stop talking. We all want to go to sleep.'

'Wait till you're head and I'll obey you, but not till then!' said Gwendoline, rather anxious to show off in front of her grand new friend. 'We'll know tomorrow who's head.'

'Well, it won't be *you*,' said Alicia's malicious voice from down the room.

'Shhhh!' said Darrell, hearing a footstep. It was Matron. She came in quietly, saw the wakeful girls, and spoke kindly to them. 'Not asleep yet? Hurry up! No more talking now, of course. Goodnight.'

She went out. Gwendoline debated whether or not to begin whispering to Daphne again. But a tiny snore from Daphne showed that she was asleep. So it wouldn't be any good to defy Sally – Daphne wouldn't be able to whisper back!

Soon all the girls were fast asleep. They didn't hear Miss Potts peep into the room and shut the door quietly. They didn't even hear the sixth-formers trooping upstairs later on. They were all tired out.

The dressing-bell awoke everyone with a jump. Sally sat straight up, startled. 'Oh – it's only the school bell,' she said, and laughed. 'I couldn't think what it was for a moment.'

The first day was always fun. No real lessons were done, though classes were held. Tests were given to see what the new girls knew. New books, pencils and so on were given out. A list of various duties was compiled, each girl taking her turn at them, week by week.

The new girls all had to go to see Miss Grayling, the quiet, low-voiced Head Mistress. She told the girls exactly the same as she had told Darrell the year before. 'You will all get a lot out of your years at Malory Towers. See that you give a lot back! Be just and responsible, kind and hardworking. I count as our successes those who leave here as young women good-hearted and kind, sensible and trustable, good sound people that the world can lean on. Our failures are those who do not learn these things in the years they are here.'

Daphne, Ellen, Belinda and all the other new girls in various forms, heard these words that morning. All of them listened, impressed. Some remembered the words and never forgot them. They would be the successes. All three new girls in the second form seemed to be listening earnestly and sincerely, especially Daphne. Miss Grayling glanced at her, looking at her closely without appearing to. She knew quite a lot about Daphne Millicent Turner.

Daphne looked back, putting all her soul into her eyes. She wanted badly to make a good impression on Miss Grayling. She smiled her charming smile, but the Head Mistress did not return it. She spoke a few more serious words and then dismissed the girls. They went silently out of the room.

'Isn't she wonderful?' said Daphne, fervently. 'Gwendoline said she'd make a real impression on me, and she has.'

Nobody appeared to care whether any impression had been made on Daphne or not. They separated and went their different ways.

This term Darrell and Sally made their way to the second-form room. They passed the door of the first-formers, the room where they themselves had sat for many terms. The door was open. A tangled crowd of small girls were choosing desks and bagging seats.

'Babies!' said Darrell, loftily. 'Just inky-fingered kids who probably don't know their twelve-times table yet.'

Two old second-formers, now third-formers, passed

them in the passage. 'Hallo, kids!' said one of the third-formers, condescendingly. 'Look out for old Nosey! She's hard on people who make too many spelling mistakes!'

Nosey was the popular name for Miss Parker, the second-form mistress. She had rather a large nose which, so the girls said, she kept putting into things that were no concern of hers. Certainly she was a most inquisitive person when she suspected any mischief was going on, and did not rest till she got to the bottom of it.

She was strict but sometimes she had dreamy fits when she seemed to forget the class and sit gazing into the distance. The class lived for these rare moments and then made the most of them. Darrell was sure she would not like Miss Parker nearly as much as she had liked Potty, the mistress who had taught her in the first form.

Belinda and Ellen seemed to be very keen to know all the details about the various teachers. Darrell and Sally were pleased to supply them. Daphne, of course, went to Gwendoline for information.

'You've got to be careful of both Mam'zelles,' said Darrell. 'But most of all of Mam'zelle Rougier, the tall thin one. They've both got tempers – but Mam'zelle Dupont's temper is just a short, hot one, and Mam'zelle Rougier's is a real *bad* one!'

'And look out for Miss Carton, the history mistress, because if you don't like history, she'll sharpen her tongue on you!' said Alicia. 'I do like it, so I'm all right. But if you don't, look out!'

The first day passed pleasantly and interestingly. The new girls were taken to see the various parts of the big school buildings, the tennis-courts, and the gardens. They marvelled at the great swimming-pool hollowed out from the rocks continually filled with fresh water each tide.

'I suppose you can swim very well,' said Daphne to Gwendoline. Gwendoline hesitated and looked round. She had been boasting quite a lot to Daphne, but not in the hearing of the others. Now Darrell was too near for her to make any untruthful statement about her swimming.

'Well – not so well as the others,' she said.

'I bet you swim the best,' said Daphne, warmly. 'You're too modest!'

Darrell giggled. No one could call Gwendoline modest, surely! She was the worst boaster in the school, and sometimes could not draw the line between stupid boasting and real untruth.

Ellen said she could not swim. 'I've never had much time for games,' she said. 'But I'd like to play them well. I've had to work so hard always.'

'You must be jolly clever,' said Mary-Lou. 'You won the only scholarship offered that would take you to Malory Towers, didn't you?'

'Yes. But I don't believe I'm *really* clever,' said Ellen, the little line deepening on her forehead and giving her a worried look. 'I mean – I can work and work and work, and remember things all right – but I'm not brilliant like some girls. Some don't need to work hard at all – they're top because they're so clever, and they can't help it. I have had to work for everything. Still – I badly wanted to come to Malory Towers, and here I am, so the hard work was worth it!'

'Well, you try being good at games as well as at work,'

said Sally, who was very keen on all games herself. 'You know what they say "All work and no play . . ." '

'Makes Jack a dull boy – and Ellen a dull girl!' said Ellen, with a small laugh. 'I'm afraid that's what I am, too – dull!'

Belinda loved everything about Malory Towers. Irene, who seemed to have taken her as much in tow as Gwendoline had taken Daphne, was delighted with Belinda's rapturous admiration of everything.

'Oh, the views!' cried Belinda. 'Look at that sea! Look at the colours in that swimming-pool! Where's my paint-box, quick!'

It was then that for the first time the girls discovered Belinda's talent. She could draw and paint marvellously well. Best of all, or so the girls thought, she could caricature anyone in a bold pencil or charcoal drawing, producing a comic exaggerated likeness that sent everyone into peals of laughter.

'We'll have some fun with you, Belinda!' said Irene. 'You can draw Nosey Parker – and Mam'zelle – both Mam'zelles, in fact – and Matron – and everyone. I'm glad you came. We'll certainly have some fun with you!'

4 Settling in

On the first day of the term Miss Parker announced who the head-girl of the form was to be. The class were all agog to hear her, and sat like mice whilst she rustled her papers and looked for her pencil.

'I am sure you all want to know who has been chosen for head-girl this term,' she said. 'Well, I will not keep you in suspense long. After a short discussion at the staff meeting we decided on – Sally Hope.'

The girls clapped and Sally blushed red. She was very pleased indeed. Miss Parker went on, glancing at her notes as she spoke.

'You may perhaps like to know what girls were in the running for the position. Darrell Rivers was, Jean MacDonald was another. Winnie Toms was a third.'

Everyone expected to hear Alicia's name mentioned, or Irene's. But Miss Parker did not give any more names at all. Irene didn't mind. She knew she was a scatter-brain and she didn't in the least want to be head of the form. So long as she had her music she was happy. Being head of the form might rob her of some of her practice time!

But Alicia did mind. She had been top of the form last term. She had a fine brain and an excellent memory, and although she never needed to work hard because she had these to help her, still she certainly had done well last term.

And yet she wasn't even in the running for the position

of head-girl! She bit her lips and wished she could stop herself going red.

'There's too much favouritism!' she told herself, fiercely. 'Just because I play the fool sometimes and upset the mistresses they won't even consider me as head!'

But Alicia was not altogether right. It was not playing the fool that made the staff pass over her name, but something else. It was Alicia's hardness to those she didn't like, her sneers at those less clever than herself, who needed help, not taunts. Often the staff laughed privately over Alicia's ridiculous tricks, and enjoyed them – but nobody liked her wild and unruly tongue, and the sharp things it could say.

'She'll get a lot of admiration and envy but she won't get much love or real friendship from others,' Miss Grayling had said at the staff meeting. 'As for Betty, her friend, she is clever too, but a little empty-head, compared with Alicia, who really has it in her to make good if she tried. It isn't Alicia's brain that is at fault, it's her heart!'

And so the choice had been made – Sally Hope, the steady, loyal, kindly, sensible Sally, Darrell's best friend. Sally might not be top of the form, but she would always listen to anyone in a difficulty. Sally would not do brilliantly in exams, as Alicia would – but she would always help a younger girl at games or lessons. She would be completely fair and just as head-girl of the form, and she wouldn't stand any nonsense.

Everyone in the form knew that a good choice had been made, although some of them would have welcomed a bad choice, for they didn't like Sally! Gwendoline was furious. So was Betty, who had hoped that Alicia would have been chosen. So were one or two of Betty's friends, not in Sally's dormy.

Darrell squeezed Sally's arm. 'Jolly good!' she said. 'I'm glad. Won't your mother be pleased? You'll be head of our dormy too, Sally. Tough for Gwendoline!'

It certainly was most annoying for Gwendoline that night in bed when Sally took command. Sally did not mean to use her new power too much or too soon, but she knew that if Gwendoline began to be silly again, she would have to make a stand at once. Gwendoline didn't understand leniency, but took advantage of it.

So, as soon as the whispering began again, after lights out, Sally spoke up.

'Shut up, Gwendoline. I told you that last night. I wasn't head of dormy then. But I am now. So shut up when I tell you.'

'Poor Daphne's homesick,' began Gwendoline.

'It won't make her any better if you whisper stuff and nonsense into her ear,' said Sally.

There was a short silence. Then Belinda's voice cut through the darkness, asking a question.

'Sally! What happens if we disobey and go on whispering when the head-girl has said we're not to?'

'Nobody ever does,' said Sally, grimly. 'But I believe there is an unwritten law at Malory Towers that if anyone makes herself a nuisance at night, the other girls must send her to Coventry.'

'Oh!' said Belinda, and snuggled down in bed, grinning to think of what Gwendoline would feel now. Would she whisper again or not?

Gwendoline had opened her mouth to continue her conversation with Daphne, but when she heard Belinda's question and its answer, she shut it again, shocked. How dare Sally hint such a thing to a second-former! She debated whether or not Sally was just saying it to scare her. But, remembering Sally's grim voice, she decided she wouldn't risk it. It would be too humiliating if Sally really did carry out her threat. Daphne would never respect her again!

So there was peace in the dormy, and when Matron came silently to the door, there was only the regular breathing of ten girls to be heard. Eight were fast asleep. But two were awake.

They were Gwendoline and Ellen. Gwendoline was cross, and that always made her wakeful. Ellen was thinking about her work. She had done fairly well in the test-papers that morning, but not brilliantly. Was she really up to the second-form work here? Oh yes, she had won that scholarship, but it wasn't brains that had done it, only hard, hard work. Was it going to be terribly hard work here to keep up with the others? Her brain didn't seem to work so easily as it used to. Ellen was worried, and did not fall asleep till long after Gwendoline.

It took the new girls a few days to get into the way of things. Ellen and Daphne learned their way about more quickly than Belinda, who kept turning up in the wrong classroom continually. She would go into the first-form classroom instead of in the second form, and Miss Potts got quite annoyed with her.

'Belinda! Don't tell me you're here *again*!' she would say. 'Do you particularly want to work with the first form? Of course, if you really feel that the work of the second form is . . .'

But by that time Belinda had fled, muttering hurried apologies. She would appear in her own form-room a minute or two late, giggling.

'I'm so sorry, I got lost, Miss Parker,' she would say, and subside into her seat.

'I'll look after her a bit, Miss Parker,' said Irene. But Miss Parker forbade that immediately.

'That would mean the two of you getting lost,' she said. 'You'd probably be down in the swimming-pool waiting for a diving lesson whilst we were all up here doing maths. It's time Belinda learned to look after herself. After all, she's been here three days now!'

'Yes, Miss Parker,' said Belinda, meekly, and began to make a little sketch of the teacher on her blotting-pad. She was always drawing, wherever she was. She kept a little sketch book in her pocket and filled it with odd drawings of the girls, the flowers on the window-sill, the view from the window, anything that caught her observant eye.

Mam'zelle Dupont, plump, short and beady-eyed, holding her lorgnettes close to her eyes, was a source of delight to Belinda, for she was so easy to draw. Nearly every girl in the class now had a neat little sketch of Mam'zelle marking her place in her French grammar. It was the ambition of the class to have, as a marker, caricatures of all the mistresses taking their different classes – Miss Carton for their history books, Miss Grayling for the scripture exercise books, Mr. Young for the school song book and so on.

Belinda had promised to do one for each girl as a marker, providing that they would tidy her drawers for her, keep her desk spick and span, and generally see that whatever she forgot, was done before she got into trouble.

'I simply can't help forgetting things,' she explained. 'I'm even worse than Irene. If I get into too many rows I get upset and can't draw. That's awful.'

'Don't worry! We'll run round you all right!' said Alicia, looking in delight at the sly drawing Belinda had done of Mr. Young the singing-master. There he was, with his funny little moustache twisted up at the ends, his bald head with the three or four hairs plastered down the middle, his too-high collar, and his eyes large behind their glasses.

'You really are a marvel, Belinda,' said Betty, looking over Alicia's shoulder at the drawing. 'What will you draw for me if I promise to take over your week of classroom duties when your turn comes?'

Thus Belinda made her bargains, and got out of all the jobs she didn't want to do! Miss Parker was amazed to find the girls doing so much for Belinda. Belinda exasperated her, with her irresponsible ways, and she couldn't think why the girls ran round her so much.

'It's odd,' she said to Mam'zelle. 'They never do that for Irene, who is almost as bad. Do they like Belinda so much then? I can't see what there is in that silly child to make them fuss round her so much! Why, I even saw *Gwendoline* tidying out her desk for her this morning, instead of going off at break!'

'Ah, Belinda has the artistic temperament!' said Mam'zelle. 'She has no time for such things as tidying

28

desks and making beds. I myself have an artistic temperament, but in this so-English school, it gets no sympathy. You English, you do not like such things.'

'No, we don't,' said Miss Parker, who had heard a good many times before about Mam'zelle Dupont's artistic temperament. It usually took the form of groaning over such laborious jobs as marking papers, making out long lists and so on. Mam'zelle's artistic temperament was always at war with such tasks, and she tried in vain to hand them over to more practical people, such as Miss Potts or Miss Parker.

'We must be patient with such as Belinda,' went on Mam'zelle. 'How I have suffered because people . . .'

'Well, believe me, Belinda will suffer too, if she doesn't get rid of some of her ways,' said Miss Parker, grimly. 'I know what Miss Potts had to put up with, in Irene, the last year. She put a bit of sense into her, thank goodness, and I can deal with her. Belinda's got to toe the line too. It's a pity all the girls seem bent on doing so much for her.'

Nobody told Miss Parker the real reason, and although she tried hard to find out, she couldn't. Nobody showed Miss Parker any of the drawings either. Belinda had a malicious pencil sometimes, and just hit off the weak points in her subjects. Miss Parker's big nose always appeared in her drawings just a *little* bit bigger than life! Mam'zelle Rougier was always bonier than she really was. Mam'zelle Dupont was rounder and fatter. No, the girls certainly didn't want to show those clever caricatures to their teachers!

The only teacher who was really delighted with

Belinda was Miss Linnie, the art-mistress. She was young and light hearted with a great sense of fun. She soon found out Belinda's gift for art, and encouraged her all she could.

'I'm going to enjoy myself here!' said Belinda to Irene. 'Miss Linnie's thrilled with me and is helping me no end. And I've got out of all the silly jobs I hate. Emily's even going to darn my stockings for me!'

'You're lucky,' said Irene, enviously. 'I wouldn't mind swopping some of my music compositions if somebody would do jobs for *me* – but nobody wants the music I write! But they all want your funny drawings, Belinda!'

5 Sorting themselves out

THE first week went slowly by. It always did go slowly, and then after that the weeks went faster and faster. All the girls had now settled in well, and were enjoying themselves.

The weather kept fine and warm and there was still bathing to be had for those who wanted it. The tennis-courts were still in use too, although the winter game of lacrosse was now being played. So there was plenty to do in spare time.

Gwendoline and Daphne had become firm friends. Gwendoline had not had a proper friend during the four terms she had been at Malory Towers and she was thrilled to have Daphne. She admired the girl's prettiness and her charming ways, and loved to hear the stories of her wealthy home.

The two girls had much in common. Neither of them liked the water and nothing would persuade them to take a dip in the pool.

'We have to do enough of that each summer,' objected Gwendoline, one hot day, when her form tried to get her to come along for a swim. 'We don't *have* to swim this term, so I'm jolly well not going to. Anyway, you don't really want me to come – all you want me for is to creep behind me and push me in!'

'No – we want Belinda to see you shivering in your bathing suit, putting one toe gingerly into the water!' said Alicia. 'It would make such a comical picture for our classroom wall, Gwendoline!'

'Beast!' said Gwendoline, who hated to be made fun of. She walked off with Daphne. 'Just because they like violent things like swimming and tennis and rough games, they think everyone ought to,' she said to Daphne. 'After all, you and I have never been to school before we came here, and we'll never get used to all their stupid ideas. I wish I had been born French. Then I shouldn't have had to swim if I didn't want to, or tire myself out trying to hit a silly ball over a net.'

'We have three courts at home,' said Daphne. 'Two are hard and one is soft. You see, Mother is a marvellous hostess, and she likes to give tennis parties as well as other kinds. But, of course, the ones people really love are the ones she gives on board Daddy's yacht.'

Gwendoline hadn't heard about the yacht before. She gazed enviously at her friend. Perhaps Daphne would invite her to stay one summer holidays and then she too could go on this wonderful yacht. How pleased her mother would be to know she had made such a fine friend at last!

'You must have hated coming away to school, Daphne,' she said. 'Leaving all your luxury, and having to pig it here. I don't expect you ever made your bed in your life before you came here.'

'Of course I didn't,' said Daphne, shaking back her pretty hair. 'And I bet you didn't either!'

'No, I didn't,' said Gwendoline. 'My governess Miss Winter always did things like that for me. She still does in the holidays. She's a stupid old-thing but she's useful in those ways. She wasn't much good at teaching me, though. I was awfully backward when I first came here.'

Gwendoline still was! Instead of getting down to things and trying to work really hard all the term to catch up with the others, she made a great show and did very little. Her parents were almost resigned to the fact that her reports always contained the words 'Fair. Could work harder.' 'Weak. Does not use her brains enough.' 'Poor – has not tried her best.'

Her father made plenty of cutting remarks about her reports, but as her mother always sympathized with Gwendoline, and spoiled her, his remarks did no good at all, except to make Gwendoline cross. Then she would burst into tears and it would be all that Miss Winter and her mother could do to comfort her. Gwendoline knew how to turn on her tears all right.

And Daphne knew how to turn on her charming smile! It got her out of a good deal of trouble, especially with Mam'zelle Dupont, Miss Linnie the art-mistress, and Mr. Young the singing-master.

Mam'zelle could not resist that smile. Daphne could make it sweet, pathetic, brave, affectionate – it was extraordinary what a smile could be!

When Daphne presented a badly written French exercise to Mam'zelle, she would turn on her smile, and Mam'zelle would gaze warmly at her. Ah, the pretty child!

'I've done my best, Mam'zelle,' Daphne would say, still keeping on her smile. 'But I'm afraid it's not very good yet. You see – it's so difficult my not having been to school before.'

Then the smile would become rather pathetic, and Mam'zelle, quite overcome, would pat Daphne's arm.

'You do your best, *mon enfant*! You cannot do more! See, I will help you if you like to come to me in the evenings for extra work!'

Mam'zelle would make this generous offer, beaming all over her face. But Daphne was quick enough to deal with it at once. She would shake her head regretfully and say how sorry she was, but already she had extra work with another mistress.

Then on would come that smile again, and the blue eyes would look beseechingly at Mam'zelle.

'Do not make me do all this French work again, please, Mam'zelle,' she would say. 'I have so much to do, to catch up with the others my first term.'

And, no matter who had their French exercises to do all over again, Daphne never did. She could do anything with Mam'zelle, if only she exerted her charm and put on that ravishing smile!

Unfortunately it worked the other way with Miss Parker, Miss Potts and Mam'zelle Rougier – especially with Mam'zelle Rougier who, as a rule, made it a habit to dislike those girls that the other Mam'zelle liked, and to like those she didn't.

She was hard on Daphne, and soon it became impossible for the girl even to try to smile at her. They both disliked one another intensely. If it had not been for the unexpected help of somebody else in the class, Daphne would have had a very bad time, and have had all her work returned from Mam'zelle Rougier.

That somebody was, surprisingly enough, Mary-Lou! Mary-Lou had become exceedingly good at French, for her mother had had a French girl to look after her in the holidays for the past year, and Mary-Lou could chatter almost as well in French now, as she could in English, pleasing both Mam'zelles immensely.

Mary-Lou thought Daphne was lovely. She couldn't help gazing and gazing at her. She would never, never like her as much as she liked Darrell and Sally, of course, but she couldn't help warming to her prettiness and nice manners.

One day she saw Daphne almost in tears over some returned work from Mam'zelle Rougier, who had told Daphne that she would return it yet again if it was not given in perfect this time. Mary-Lou went to her.

'Can't Gwendoline help you?' she asked timidly. 'She's

not doing anything in particular. Shall I ask her to come and help you?'

Daphne dabbed her eyes and turned a watery but still charming smile on Mary-Lou. 'No, it's no good asking Gwen. She'd help if she could. But she's not much better than I am at French!'

'Well – I suppose you wouldn't like *me* to help you, would you?' asked Mary-Lou, eagerly. 'I'd like to.'

'Oh, thanks awfully,' said Daphne, thrilled. 'You're frightfully good at it, I know. Simply wizard. Look, what have I done wrong here?'

Mary-Lou slipped happily into a seat beside Daphne and began to explain a few things to her. Without realizing it she had soon done the whole of the work, and Daphne smiled to herself, and thanked Mary-Lou warmly.

'That's all right,' said Mary-Lou, shyly. She gazed at Daphne's curling golden hair. 'You've got beautiful hair,' she said.

Daphne was like Gwen. She loved people to admire her and say nice things. She looked at little Mary-Lou and quite liked her. Also she thought it would be extremely useful if Mary-Lou would always help her with her French.

'I suppose you wouldn't give me a hand with my French sometimes, would you?' she asked. 'I don't want any extra coaching from either of the Mam'zelles, but I'd love to let you explain things to me. You explain very well.'

Nobody had ever asked Mary-Lou for help before in that way. She went brilliant red, and swallowed hard.

'I'd love to,' she said at last. 'Fancy *me* helping *you*!

35

I'm the one that's usually always rushing round for help. I'd love to, Daphne.'

So, to the astonishment of the second-formers, they saw the curious sight of little Mary-Lou sitting by Daphne in the evenings at the end of the common-room, carefully explaining the mistakes made in the French exercise of the day before!

'*And* doing all the next day's work for her too!' said Darrell, in disgust. She didn't like to see the faithful Mary-Lou sitting so long with somebody else. Why, Mary-Lou had tagged along behind Darrell and Sally for terms and terms! Surely she wasn't going to make that awful Daphne her friend.

'Let her be,' said the sensible Sally. 'If she wants to help her, why not? Daphne is awful at French, but I don't blame her for not taking extra coaching from the Mam'zelles. You know how irritable Mam'zelle Rougier gets in the evening, and you know how long Mam'zelle Dupont keeps you if you do go for extra work. You're supposed to go for half an hour and she keeps you two hours!'

'I hope Daphne won't put any of her silly ideas into Mary-Lou's head,' said Darrell.

'Maybe Mary-Lou will put a few *sensible* ideas into Daphne's head,' said Sally. 'I know you're longing to interfere, Darrell. Well, don't!'

The girls soon sorted themselves out in the form, making their own friends, choosing people to sit next to and go for walks with. It was nice to have a particular friend, and to have someone to confide in.

Sally had Darrell and Darrell had Sally. Irene had

Belinda. The two became quite inseparable, and did one another no good. What one forgot the other certainly didn't remember! They seemed to make one another worse.

Alicia, of course, had Betty. Alicia was not as good tempered as usual. She still smarted because she had not been made head-girl, and she was not at all nice to Sally nor as loyal to her as she should have been. Sally took no notice, but she was not very happy about it.

Gwen had Daphne, of course – and now Mary-Lou seemed to want Daphne too! How was Gwen going to feel about that?

'You needn't worry,' said Daphne to Gwen. 'I'm only using her, silly little thing! I'll let her come out with me sometimes, when you're busy, because I don't want her to think I only want her help for my French. You can use her too, Gwen. Copy my work when I've done it!'

So Gwendoline put up with Mary-Lou's company at times, and even said nothing when she went off alone with Daphne. What did it matter? Daphne was only using her!

But all the same Daphne couldn't help liking little Mary-Lou – and it was certainly a change from the silly Gwen to have good-hearted Mary-Lou trotting by her side once or twice a week!

6 The invisible chalk

After a few weeks Alicia got restless. 'It's time we livened things up a bit!' she said to Betty. 'I know we're second-formers now and all that – but there's no reason why we shouldn't have a bit of fun. Sally's such a bore – never a joke, never a trick!'

'What shall we do?' said Betty, her wicked dark eyes gleaming. 'I've got some invisible chalk. Have you got anything?'

'Invisible chalk! You never told me!' said Alicia, her face brightening. 'What is it? Show me!'

'I've got it in my locker, in a box,' said Betty. 'The common-room will be empty now. Come along and I'll show you. It's weird stuff.'

The two girls went to their common-room. Betty opened her locker and took out a tin box. Inside, wrapped carefully in paper, was a thick slab of curious pink chalk.

'It doesn't look invisible!' said Alicia. 'What does it do?'

'Well, if you rub it on to a chair, it can't possibly be seen,' said Betty. 'And whoever sits down on it makes it warm and it leaves a bright pink patch on a dress or skirt.'

'I see,' said Alicia. 'Golly – we could rub it on the mistress's chair in our form-room – when Mam'zelle Rougier is coming perhaps.'

'I know! Let's rub it on to Mr. Young's chair, when he comes to take singing!' said Betty. 'On his piano stool! Then he'll sit down hard on it when he plays the accompaniment for our songs – and when he gets up and turns round to write on the blackboard – golly, what a scream!'

Alicia laughed loudly. 'It would be better to play it on Mr. Young than on Nosey or Mam'zelle – he won't suspect a thing – and the first form will have a share in the joke too, because they take singing with us!'

Alicia cheered up considerably after this. She and Betty tried out the invisible chalk very carefully, and it was a great success.

Betty took a wooden-bottomed chair and rubbed the curious pink chalk all over it. 'Look,' she said, 'it doesn't show at all, Alicia. Can you see anything of it?'

Alicia looked carefully at the chair, tipping it this way and that. 'It's perfect,' she said. 'Not a thing to be seen! Funny how you can rub it on and it seems to disappear, Betty. It really is invisible. Now, you sit down on it and let me see what happens.'

Betty sat down, and remained there for a minute or two. The chalk would not work unless it was slightly warmed. As Betty was sitting solemnly there with Alicia watching her, Gwendoline popped her head in to look for Daphne. She was astonished to see Betty sitting solemnly by herself on a chair, with Alicia a little way off.

'What are you doing?' she asked curiously. 'What's happening?'

'Nothing,' said Alicia. 'Buzz off! Daphne's not here.'

'But what are you *doing*?' persisted Gwendoline, suspecting something, though she didn't know what. 'Why is Betty sitting on that uncomfortable chair in the middle of the room like that?'

'Alicia! Nosey wants you!' suddenly cried a voice, and Jean's head came round the door. 'Hurry! She's in a stew about something. Your maths paper, I should think.'

'Blow!' said Alicia, and shot off. 'Be back in a minute, Betty,' she said, and ran down the passage. Jean looked with interest at Betty sitting all alone in the middle of the common-room.

'Tired?' she asked. Betty scowled. She felt foolish. She wanted to hurl a book at Gwendoline's silly golden head, but she didn't dare to get up in case she had a nice chalky pattern on her back. She didn't want to let anyone else into the trick at the moment.

'Paralysed or something, poor thing,' said Gwendoline. 'Can't get up. Or perhaps it's rheumatism!'

To Betty's great relief Gwendoline became tired of teasing her and went out to find Daphne. Jean gave a grin and left too. Betty got up and looked round at herself. She gave a chuckle of delight. She had a brilliant pink pattern on the skirt of her tunic. How extraordinary that the invisible chalk should act like that when it was warmed up!

Alicia came flying in. 'Does it work?' she cried, and giggled when Betty swung round and showed her the bright pink marks. 'Golly, it's fine! We'll try it on old Mr. Young tomorrow!'

'Shall we tell anyone?' asked Betty.

'Not a soul,' said Alicia. 'Someone's sure to give it away by giggling if we do. No – we'll let dear Mr. Young spring this surprise himself on an astonished audience!'

Neither Betty nor Alicia did much prep that night. Potty, who was taking prep, looked with suspicion at the two plotters and wondered what was up. It was obvious that their thoughts were pleasantly and humorously engaged far elsewhere.

Potty knew the signs. She warned Miss Parker. 'Those two in your form, Alicia and Betty, are up to something, Miss Parker. Look out tomorrow. You'll have an unaccountable smell, or a curious noise, or an orgy of book-dropping or something.'

'Thanks,' said Miss Parker, grimly. 'I'll watch out.'

But she could see nothing out of the way in her first lesson, or in her second one either. The girls worked much as usual. Only Alicia and Betty seemed restless. But then they often were, especially Alicia, whose quick mind often chafed at the slower rate of the others.

The lesson before break was singing. Just before the second lesson was finished Betty put up her hand. 'Please, Miss Parker, it's my turn to get things ready for Mr. Young in the singing-room. May I go?'

Miss Parker glanced at the clock. 'Yes. You have about four minutes.'

Betty flashed a quick grin at Alicia and went demurely to the door. Once outside she raced down the corridor and made her way to the singing-room. No one was there. Mr. Young was always a minute or two late, thank goodness!

Betty flew to the piano stool. It was the round leather-topped kind, that could be screwed round and round. Betty took out her piece of pink chalk and rubbed it vigorously all over the top of the round stool.

She was sure there was not a single spot unchalked though, of course, she could not see anything of what she had done at all. It certainly was invisible chalk!

Then she quickly sent the stool spinning round till it was too low for Mr. Young. If ever it was too low or too high he had a little habit of sitting on the stool and going round and round with it till it had reached the height he liked. If only he did that today it would give the chalk a wonderful chance of getting properly on to him!

Betty stacked the music ready and cleaned the blackboard. Then there came the sound of feet and the first form marched into the room under the sharp eye of Miss Potts.

Then came the second form. Alicia's eyes were bright. Betty grinned at her and winked. Then she went to hold the door for the two mistresses to go out and for Mr. Young to come in.

In he trotted, a dapper little man in a well-brushed black suit and a too-high collar. He smoothed his pointed moustache and bowed politely to the girls.

'Good morning, young ladies.'

'Good morning, Mr. Young,' they chorused, and rustled their song-sheets. The lesson began. Mr. Young took some blackboard drill for five minutes, explaining various notes and signs. Then he went to the piano.

Betty nudged Alicia and held her breath. But, most annoyingly, Mr. Young did not sit down. He struck a few notes with one hand, standing facing the girls as he did so, his baton raised.

'Exercises, please,' he said. 'I wish to see your mouths well open, and to hear the sound coming from the back of the throat.'

Mr. Young set great store on the Back of the Throat. It was always coming into everything, exercises, songs and sight-reading. Back of the Throat was his one unfailing motto.

Now he stood, instead of sitting, and conducted the exercises. Alicia was in agonies of disappointment. Suppose he didn't sit down at all? Probably the next person then to sit down would be the accompanist of the mistress who taught dancing – and she always wore a brightly coloured frock so that the chalk wouldn't show at all! What a waste!

But Mr. Young did sit down eventually, of course. He had a new song to teach to the girls and, as always, he wanted to play the whole thing through two or three times before he taught it, so that the girls could catch the lilt and swing and tune of it.

So down he sat. Aha! That stool was once more too low! Mr. Young twirled himself vigorously round on it till it was the right height. The girls giggled. Mr. Young could never realize how funny he was, twirling round lightly on that little stool.

'Now I will play you your new song,' said Mr. Young. 'You may sit to listen to it. You will hear when the chorus comes, for I will sing it to you.'

Off he started, tumty-tum-ti-tum, his hands flying up and down, and then his voice booming out at the chorus. Alicia and Betty winked at one another. The chalk ought to be working now!

Three times Mr. Young played the song and then he got up. 'Did you like it?' he asked, and the girls chorused loudly. 'Oh, *yes*, Mr. Young!'

Mr. Young turned towards the blackboard and picked up a piece of white chalk. At once the girls saw that he was smeared with the brightest imaginable pink at the back! They stared in delight.

'Look at Mr. Young! What's he rubbed against? Oh, do look!'

Soon the class was in a state of giggles and Mr. Young glared round.

'Silence, please! What behaviour is this today?'

There was a momentary silence, but as soon as the unfortunate singing-master turned back to the board again more giggles broke out. Then Irene gave one of her terrific explosions.

Mr. Young flung the chalk down on the floor. He looked as if he was about to stamp on it, and probably he would have done so if the door hadn't suddenly opened, and Miss Grayling appeared. She had someone with her.

'Oh, excuse me for interrupting your class, Mr. Young,' she said. 'But could you just have a word with Mr. Lemming about the piano here?'

Mr. Young had to swallow his annoyance and explain what was wrong with the piano. In doing so he turned his back to Miss Grayling who eyed his patch of brilliant pink with the utmost astonishment. The girls were as quiet as mice now, and Alicia and Betty felt distinctly anxious.

Miss Grayling turned to Sally, the head of the second form. 'Will you go to the hall and fetch the clothes brush there?' she said. 'Poor Mr. Young has brushed against something.'

Sally flew off and fetched the brush. Mr. Young was surprised to hear Miss Grayling's remark. He looked over his shoulder trying to see himself.

44

'Is it paint?' he asked in alarm. 'I do hope not! Oh – only chalk! How in the world did it get there?'

7 'Oy!'

Soon the offending pink chalk had been vigorously brushed away by Mr. Lemming, who then proceeded to sit down on the piano stool himself to try out some of the bass notes, which had gone wrong. Alicia and Betty watched breathlessly. Most of the girls, guessing that some trick was being played, watched eagerly too.

They were well rewarded when Mr. Lemming rose from the stool. He was wearing a long black overcoat and on it was a wonderful pattern of bright pink. Mr. Young stared at it in amazement.

'Ah, you have it too!' he cried. 'See, Miss Grayling, Mr. Lemming has brushed up against something also. I will soon put him right.'

In spite of being under Miss Grayling's eye the girls began to giggle. Miss Grayling looked very puzzled.

'Your coat was quite all right when we came along here,' she said to Mr. Lemming. 'I am sure I should have noticed it if you had brushed against anything so violently pink as this. In any case there is no wall as pink as this chalk! Whatever can have happened?'

She walked to the stool and looked at it very closely.

Alicia and Betty hardly dared to breathe. But the invisible chalk lived up to its name and Miss Grayling did not see a sign of it. It did not occur to her to sit down and see if the same thing happened to her. Still feeling puzzled she took Mr. Lemming out of the room, and the lesson proceeded again.

Not until the end of it did poor Mr. Young sit down on that stool again. When he got up, behold! He was as pretty a sight as before, and the girls stuffed their hankies into their mouths trying not to explode with mirth. Mr. Young noticed nothing this time. He walked pompously to the door and gave the girls the quick little bow he always kept for them.

'Good morning, young ladies!' And out he went, showing his patch of brilliant colour. As he went the bell for break rang, and the girls tore into the Court, longing to give way to their pent-up laughter.

'Alicia! You had something to do with it! *What* was it?'

'Oh, it was marvellous! When he turned round to the blackboard I thought I should die!'

'Betty! Do tell! Was it your trick? How did you do it? I looked at the stool and there wasn't a thing to be seen!'

'That reminds me,' said Betty to Alicia with a grin. 'I must get a wet cloth and rub it over the stool.' She disappeared, and the girls surged round Alicia, begging her to tell them the secret.

Meanwhile Mr. Young was walking down one of the long corridors, quite unaware of his beautiful decoration. Mam'zelle Dupont happened to come out of a room just behind him, and stared disbelievingly at the

extraordinary sight. She raced after him.

'Monsieur Young! Ha, Monsieur Young!'

Mr. Young was scared of both Mam'zelles. He hastened his steps. Mam'zelle ran more quickly.

'Monsieur, Monsieur, *attendez, je vous prie*! Wait, wait. You cannot go out like that! It is terrible!'

Mr. Young swung round, annoyed. 'What is it? What's terrible?'

'This! This!' said Mam'zelle, and tapped him smartly on the chalk. A cloud of it flew off at once. Mr. Young was horrified at being tapped so familiarly by Mam'zelle and amazed at the cloud of chalk that flew from his person. He wriggled himself round to try and see it, remembering what Mr. Lemming's coat had been like.

'I will attend to you,' said Mam'zelle, out of the kindness of her heart, and caught hold of his arm. She hurried him to a hall-stand, took up a brush there, and with extremely vigorous strokes she removed the chalk from his clothes.

He was angry and not at all grateful. 'Twice it has happened this morning,' he said angrily to Mam'zelle and actually shook his fist in her face as if she was the culprit. She backed away, alarmed. Mr. Young snatched up his hat and went off, muttering to himself.

'He is not polite, that man,' said Mam'zelle to herself. 'I do him a kindness, and he puts his fist into my face. I will never speak to him again.'

The only girl who had seen this episode in the hall was Darrell, and she hurried to the others with the tit-bit. 'I was going past the end of the hall and I saw Mam'zelle banging at Mr. Young for all she was worth with the

48

clothes brush,' she panted. 'He was so angry! Oh, do let's do it again, Alicia. It's a gorgeous trick!'

It is always a mistake to play the same trick twice running, and Alicia knew it. But she could not resist the temptation to try it on Mam'zelle Dupont.

'Shall we?' she asked Betty, and Betty nodded in glee. The girls crowded round to see the strange invisible chalk. They chuckled and laughed when they thought of the singing-lesson, and they let the first-formers into the secret too.

Altogether the trick cheered up everyone considerably, and the thought that they would play it once more gave them something to look forward to.

'Who can rub it on the mistress's chair before the French lesson this afternoon?' demanded Betty. 'Alicia and I can't. We've no chance of being in the room. Who is room monitor?'

'I am,' said Darrell. 'I'll do it! Give me the chalk! What do you do? Just rub it over the chair?'

Ten minutes before afternoon school Darrell slipped into the second-form classroom. It was her job that week to tidy the bookshelves, clean the blackboard and see that the chalk was handy and the duster there.

It took her only a minute to do these things. Then she went to the chair that stood behind the desk and took the chalk from her pocket. She was about to rub it over the seat of the chair when a mischievous idea struck her.

Couldn't she write something short so that a word would appear on Mam'zelle's skirt, and send everyone into fits? It would have to be a short word.

'I'll write "OY!" ' said Darrell to herself, in glee. 'I'll

49

have to write it backwards, so that it will come off on Mam'zelle the right way round.'

So, very painstakingly she rubbed the chalk on the seat of the chair in the form of the letters O and Y! OY! Fancy going about with that written on you! How all the girls would yell.

The bell went for lessons. Darrell slipped the chalk into her pocket and went to her place. She giggled when the rest of the form came in.

'Did you do it? Did you have time?' whispered the girls. Darrell nodded. Then in came Mam'zelle, appearing to be in quite a good temper, and the door was shut.

Mam'zelle sat down at once. She had very tiny feet and did not like standing. The girls watched eagerly. When would she stand up? Darrell could hardly wait for her to turn her back to the class. What would they say when they saw what she had written on the chair!

Jean was called to the blackboard to write something. 'Do it all wrong!' hissed Darrell. 'Then Mam'zelle will get up to correct it.'

So, much to Mam'zelle's surprise, the usually careful Jean made ridiculous mistakes in the French words she wrote down, and appeared to be quite unable to put them right, despite Mam'zelle's exasperated instructions. At last, thoroughly annoyed, she dismissed Jean to her seat, and got up to put the mistakes right herself.

The class saw her back view at once, and gasped. Written across her tight-fitting skirt in bright pink letters was the word 'OY!' Even Darrell was surprised to see it so clearly, and suddenly felt very uncomfortable. It was one thing to make a patch of pink appear on somebody's clothes – it could easily be explained away – but how could the word 'OY!' be explained? It was quite impossible.

The class gaped at Mam'zelle's back view. They were absolutely taken aback. They didn't know whether to giggle or to be alarmed.

'Darrell! You idiot! Suppose she goes walking up the corridor in front of all the other mistresses with that written on her skirt!' hissed Alicia. 'Really, you might have more sense.'

The thought of the other mistresses seeing Mam'zelle's 'OY!' really alarmed the form. Miss Parker would certainly not approve. She would consider it most disrespectful.

But how to get it off? That dreadful pink 'OY!' flashed back and forth as Mam'zelle wrote on the board, turned to the class to explain, and wrote again.

'I'll tell Mam'zelle she's got some dust or something on her skirt and I'll brush it off,' promised Darrell, in a whisper. 'At the end of the lesson.'

But she had no chance to, for Mam'zelle walked off in a hurry, remembering that she was late for the first form, next door. And the first-formers had the surprise of their lives when they saw Mam'zelle's pink 'OY!' flashing at them every other minute!

They couldn't keep back their giggles and Mam'zelle grew more and more furious. 'What is there so funny about me this afternoon?' she demanded. 'Is my hair untidy? Is there mud on my face? Are my shoes not a pair?'

'No, Mam'zelle,' said the first form, almost helpless with trying to stop their laughter.

'I am not funny and I do not feel funny,' said Mam'zelle, severely. 'But I shall soon do some funny things. Ah, yes! I shall soon say, "One hundred lines of French poetry from you, please, and from you and you!" Aha! I shall soon be very funny!'

With that she swung round to the blackboard and the 'OY!' flashed again. The first form clutched one another in agonies of suppressed laughter.

But all the same they had the sense to grab Mam'zelle before she went out of the room. 'We'll have to get that off her before she goes,' said Hilda. 'Or else the second-formers will get into awful trouble. I expect they meant to brush it off somehow and didn't have the chance.'

So, before Mam'zelle left the first-form room, Hilda politely offered to brush down her skirt, as it was all dusty with chalk.

'*Tiens*!' said Mam'zelle, looking down at it. 'This blackboard chalk! It is not good for dresses. Thank you, Hilda, *vous êtes gentille*! You are kind.'

She stood like a lamb whilst Hilda assiduously brushed her skirt back and front, and got rid of the pink 'OY!' Then she walked out of the room. The second-formers, who had finished their lesson, were watching for her, hoping to brush her down themselves before she went off to the little room she shared with Miss Potts.

With great relief they saw that Mam'zelle's skirt was now spotless. They went back into their form-room and sank down into their chairs.

'Thank goodness!' said Alicia. 'We might have got into a first-class row over that. Potty or Nosey would certainly have reported it if they'd seen that "OY!" You

52

know how annoyed the mistresses get if they think we've been really disrespectful, Darrell. You were an idiot. I suppose Sally put you up to it. Fine head of form she is!'

'Shut up!' said Darrell, annoyed with herself and everyone else too. 'Sally had nothing to do with it. I just didn't think, that's all!'

8 The term goes on

The affair of the invisible chalk was talked about for days afterwards. Some of the upper school got to hear about it, and secretly wished they too could have seen Mam'zelle's 'OY!' Those in the know grinned at Darrell when they met her, and whispered 'OY!' into her ear!

It seemed as if everyone thought that the whole idea was Darrell's and Alicia and Betty were annoyed about it. Why should Darrell get all the credit, when all she had done was to make that word appear on Mam'zelle's skirt, and risk getting the whole of the form into very serious trouble?

The two of them cold-shouldered Darrell, and Darrell retaliated by ignoring them as much as she could. She knew that Alicia was still sore about not being head-girl, and was not being nice to Sally. Darrell was loyal, and she was not going to have that if she could help it!

Alicia's tongue grew wild and sharp again. Darrell,

knowing that Alicia was trying to make her lose her temper, grew red with suppressed rage, but said nothing. She mustn't lose her temper, she mustn't! If she did she would begin to shout, she might even throw something at Alicia – and then she would put herself in the wrong immediately. So she looked as if she was going to burst, but didn't.

And it was very bad for her. Sally tried to calm her down, but that made Darrell worse.

'Don't you see that it's because you're my friend that I get so wild with Alicia?' Darrell would say. 'She could say all she liked about me, I wouldn't care – but it's hard to sit and listen to things about *you*, Sally. All because she's jealous. She just says them because she knows I've got a temper and want to stick up for you.'

'Well, for goodness' sake don't go and fall into her trap,' said the sensible Sally. 'That would be idiotic. She and Betty would have the laugh over you easily.'

So poor Darrell had to grit her teeth and say nothing when Alicia and Betty had one of their cross-talk conversations to bait her.

'*Dear* Sally!' Alicia would say. 'Always so good – and yet so dull. The Perfect Head-Girl. Don't you think so, Betty?'

'Oh, I do so agree with you,' Betty would say, with a smile that infuriated Darrell. 'Think what a good example she is to us all – dear, conscientious Sally. Really, I feel overcome with shame at my faults when I see Sally sitting so prim and good in class. Not a joke, not a smile. *Such* a model for all of us!'

'What *should* we do without her?' Alicia would go on,

glancing slyly at Darrell to see if she was at bursting point yet. If Darrell got up and went away, the two counted it as a victory for them – but poor Darrell knew quite well that if she stayed much longer, her mouth would open and she would say things she would regret bitterly afterwards.

So Darrell's temper was not too good those days. And there was someone else whose temper was not good either. And that was Ellen's.

She had been quite even-tempered, though rather worried-looking for the first few weeks. And then suddenly she became really irritable. She snapped at the girls, and the little cleft in her forehead deepened until it seemed as if she was always frowning.

Jean tried to find out if anything was the matter. Sally had tried, but Ellen seemed to think that Sally was just being a good head-girl, trying to set her right and stop her being so irritable. So she snapped at Sally, and the head-girl, surprised and hurt, said no more.

'Funny girl!' she said to Darrell. 'I don't understand her. She's won a scholarship to Malory Towers which must mean she's terribly clever – and she works as hard or harder than any of us do – and yet she's never top, or even in the first three or four! I suppose she's cross about that and gets bad tempered. I don't like her.'

'Neither do I,' said Darrell. 'She's not worth bothering about, Sally. Leave her alone.'

'Oh, I think she's worth bothering about,' said Sally. 'Everybody is. I'll ask Jean to have a word with her. She sits next to her in class.'

Jean was a very forthright girl, with little imagination, and usually went at things in the way a tank might, crushing all resistance, insisting on knowing what she wanted to know. But for some reason she did not tackle Ellen quite in this way. She sat next to her in class and she slept next to her in the dormy – so she had had plenty of opportunity of hearing Ellen's unconscious sighs and little groans when she was hard at work – or when she was trying to go to sleep!

She knew that Ellen often lay awake at night, and she guessed that Ellen was worrying about something. It couldn't be her work, surely – no scholarship girl needed to worry about work! As far as she had seen, all scholarship girls found work very easy indeed.

Jean was a kindly girl, though sometimes much too blunt in her speech and ways. She tried to think how to get at Ellen. There didn't seem any way except by asking her straight out what was the matter, and couldn't it be put right?

But that just wouldn't do. Ellen would snap at once, as she did to Sally. So, for once, Jean gave the matter some thought, and did not act as clumsily as she usually did.

Ellen had no friend. She did not encourage anyone at all, not even the quiet Emily. Jean set herself out to be friendly in unobtrusive ways. She would never be able to force out of Ellen what was the matter – but perhaps she could persuade the girl to trust her enough to want to tell her! This was really a very praiseworthy idea on Jean's part, for it was seldom that the blunt Scots girl bothered herself to go to a lot of trouble in her dealings with people.

But she was rather proud that Sally had asked her to try her hand at Ellen, as she herself had failed. So, although Ellen did not realize it at the time, Jean set herself out to be kind and helpful in all kinds of little ways.

She helped Ellen to hunt for ages for her gym shoes which were lost. She sympathized when the photograph of Ellen's parents got broken, and offered to get some glass cut for the frame, when next she went to the shops. She helped her to dry her hair when she washed it. Just little things that nobody, not even Ellen at first, noticed very much.

But gradually Ellen grew to trust this shrewd Scots girl. She told her when she had a very bad headache, although she refused to go to Matron and tell her too. She stopped snapping at Jean, though she still snapped at everyone else – except Mary-Lou. It would need a very hard-hearted, bad-tempered person to snap at little Mary-Lou!

There were some evenings when Ellen was quite unbearable. 'Really, anyone would think she suffered from what my mother calls "Nerves",' said Alicia, one evening. 'Jumps at any little thing, takes things the wrong way, snaps like a bad dog – look at her now, scowling at her work-basket as if it had bitten her!'

If anyone passed too close to Ellen and knocked her elbow, she would jump and snap, 'Look out! Can't you see where you're going?'

If anyone interrupted her reading, she would slam her book down on the table and glare at the offender. 'Can't you see I'm reading? There isn't a quiet place in the whole of this beastly house!'

'You're not reading,' Darrell would say. 'You haven't

turned a page since you took up your book!'

'Oh – so you've been watching me, have you?' Ellen would say, and her eyes would suddenly fill with tears. Then she would go out of the room and slam the door.

'Isn't she awful! Scratches like a cat!'

'I wish she'd won a scholarship to somewhere else!'

'Always pretending to read and study and yet she slides down lower every week! Hypocrite, I call her!'

'Och, she's not a happy girl! Maybe she hasn't settled down here yet!' That was Jean, of course, and Sally would flash her a glance of approval. Jean certainly had an uphill task with Ellen, but she was persevering with it!

The weather was bad just then, and there was no lacrosse, and not even a walk, for the country round about was deep in mud. The girls grew restless, penned up indoors, and the teachers decided that, bad weather or not, there had better be a School Walk the next day.

Everyone groaned. The rain poured down. The sky was black and lowering. The lacrosse fields were half under water. Whatever would the country lanes be like? The sea was an angry grey-green, and the wind was so high on the cliff that no girl was allowed up there in case she was blown over.

Gwendoline and Daphne grumbled the loudest of all. Gwendoline developed a persistent sniff in class, hoping that Miss Parker would think she had a cold and let her off the walk. But Miss Parker had been warned by Potty of Gwendoline's sniffs, and was not sympathetic.

'If you want to sniff anymore, you can go and do it outside the door,' she said. 'If there's one thing I cannot bear, it's somebody sniffing. It's disgusting, it's unnecessary, and in your case, it is probably put on, Gwendoline.'

Gwendoline glared. Why were there no school teachers like her old governess at home, Miss Winter? She always rushed for a thermometer at once, if Gwendoline so much as cleared her throat, and would never, never dream of making her go out for a walk in such terrible weather!

She did not dare to sniff again, and was annoyed at Darrell's grins. Daphne looked at her sympathetically. Not that she cared whether Gwendoline had a cold or not, but it was the thing to do – Gwendoline simply lapped up sympathy.

Daphne herself tried other tactics to get out of the walk. She had no intention at all of wading through miles of mud. She went to Mam'zelle Dupont with her exercise book that evening. She put on her sweetest smile and knocked at the door of the little room which Miss Potts shared with Mam'zelle. She hoped fervently that Potty wasn't there. Potty always seemed to be irritated by Daphne's presence.

Fortunately Potty wasn't there. 'Ah, it is you, *ma petite* Daphne!' cried Mam'zelle, welcoming her favourite with a smile almost as charming as Daphne's. 'You have something to say to me? You do not understand something, is it not?'

'Oh, Mam'zelle, I'm in such a muddle over these tenses,' said Daphne. 'I really do feel that I ought to have a little extra coaching in them, if you could possibly spare the time. I do so badly want to get my French better.'

'But it has been much better lately, my dear child!' cried Mam'zelle, beaming, not knowing that little Mary-

Lou had been doing most of Daphne's French for her. 'I am pleased with you.'

Daphne turned on her smile again and Mam'zelle's heart melted still further. Ah, this pretty Daphne! She put her arm round her. 'Yes, yes, of course I will give you a little extra coaching,' she said. 'We shall soon put these tenses right. You can stay now, *ma petite*?'

'No, not now, Mam'zelle,' said Daphne. 'But I could give up that lovely country walk tomorrow, if you would be good enough to take me then. It's the only spare time I have.'

'The good child – to give up the walk that you English girls so dearly love!' cried Mam'zelle, who thought that all walks were an extremely silly invention. 'Yes, I can take you then. I will tell Miss Parker. You are a good girl, Daphne. I am pleased with you!'

'Thank you, Mam'zelle,' said Daphne, delighted, and gave Mam'zelle a ravishing smile as she went triumphantly out of the room.

9   Daphne is annoyed

Miss Parker was surprised and annoyed when she heard that Daphne was not to go with the class on their long walk. She looked crossly at Mam'zelle.

'But why this sudden desire for French on Daphne's

part?' she said. 'She's just the type of girl that needs a jolly good long walk – yes, and a muddy one too. Shake some of her airs and graces off her! Give her the extra lesson another time, Mam'zelle.'

But Mam'zelle was obstinate. She did not like Miss Parker, with her big nose. She pursed up her small mouth and shook her head. 'I cannot take Daphne any other time. It is good of the girl to give up a nice walk to improve her French.'

Miss Parker made a disbelieving noise that irritated Mam'zelle at once. 'She wants to get out of the walk, you know that perfectly well, Mam'zelle. It's foolish to give her her way like that! Daphne gets her way too easily, and I don't like some of her methods. Too under-hand for me!'

Mam'zelle stood up for her favourite, and began to exaggerate. 'Miss Parker! If you knew how much that girl wanted to go for her walk! Ah, to splash through the autumn lanes! Ah, to sniff the sea air after being cooped up so long! Daphne has sacrificed her pleasure, and she should be praised for that, not blamed. She will be hard at work with me whilst you are all enjoying yourselves out in the lovely air.'

'Well, she wouldn't take Mam'zelle Rougier in quite so easily as she takes *you*,' said Miss Parker, beginning to lose her temper. '*She* sees through her all right!'

Mam'zelle began to bristle. 'I will have a word with Mam'zelle Rougier,' she began. 'I will have two, three, four words. She shall not say things about Daphne, who is getting so much better at French!'

'Let's drop the subject,' said Miss Parker, feeling

heartily tired of Daphne. 'Go and have it out with Mam'zelle Rougier if you like. I don't care! Except that I feel Daphne has got the better of us, I'm glad not to have her with us on the walk, moaning and groaning, dragging her feet along!'

Daphne could not resist telling everyone of the way she had managed to get out of the walk. Gwendoline wished she had been sharp enough to do the same. The others were frankly disgusted with the hypocritical little trick.

'Fancy doing all that just to get out of going for a walk!' said Darrell. 'It'll be fun, splashing through the puddles in our Wellingtons. Well – if you *want* to spend the afternoon doing French verbs, good luck to you! That's just like you, somehow, Daphne.'

But, the walk didn't come off after all! The wind blew itself into a gale, and Miss Parker decided that it must be put off. The girls were just putting on their macs and Wellingtons when she came to the cloakroom to tell them. Daphne had already taken her French book to Mam'zelle.

'Girls! I'm sorry! But the wind has become a perfect gale!' said Miss Parker, appearing suddenly in the cloak-room. 'The walk is off. But to make up, we'll all go into the gym and have an afternoon of riotous games, shall we? And I'll get Matron to let us have a picnic tea in there, to make a change, if some of you will carry in the stuff.'

The girls cheered. An afternoon of jolly games – racing round, competing with one another, laughing, yelling – and ending up with a picnic tea on the floor. That certainly would be a change!

Matron came up to scratch too – she provided four super chocolate cakes for a treat, as well as two pots of golden honey. The girls were thrilled.

'What about Daphne, Miss Parker?' said Mary-Lou, remembering that Daphne was with Mam'zelle. 'Shall I go and fetch her?'

'Idiot!' said Alicia, under her breath. 'Fancy reminding Miss Parker of Daphne! Serve her right to miss all this! I'll tell Mary-Lou what I think of her in a minute!'

Miss Parker looked down at Mary-Lou's anxious face, and wondered for the twentieth time why Mary-Lou bothered about Daphne when she had Darrell and Sally for friends.

'Oh, Mary-Lou, no, you mustn't disturb Daphne!' said Miss Parker, clearly, so that all the listening girls heard quite well. 'She badly wanted to have this extra coaching, Mam'zelle tells me, and was quite willing to forgo the walk. She would be willing to forgo the games and picnic too, I am sure. We mustn't disturb her. When a girl shows herself to be as studious as that it would be a pity to spoil it all.'

Mary-Lou was the only one who did not see the sly humour of Miss Parker's words. The others did immediately, and a roar of laughter broke out. Miss Parker smiled too.

'Tough for Daphne!' said Alicia. 'Serves her jolly well right!'

They had a fun and riotous afternoon, and got thoroughly tired and dusty. Then they sat down to an enormous tea, demolishing bread and butter and honey and the four chocolate cakes in no time.

Daphne appeared just as the last piece of cake was eaten. She had had an extremely boring afternoon, for Mam'zelle Dupont had taken her at her word and had given her some very, very thorough coaching in the French verbs. She had made poor Daphne repeat them after her scores of times, she had corrected her pronunciation conscientiously, she had even made her write them out.

Daphne wished hearily she had never suggested such a thing. She had thought that she would have had a nice cosy time with Mam'zelle, talking about herself. But although Mam'zelle was fond of Daphne and quite taken in by her, she was determined to do her duty as regards coaching the girl. So she kept poor Daphne's nose to the grindstone, and when Daphne faintly protested, saying that she thought she had bothered Mam'zelle enough and the girls would be back from their walk now, surely, Mam'zelle pooh-poohed the idea at once.

'We shall hear the girls come back,' she said, not knowing that they had never gone out. 'As soon as we hear them, you shall go down to join them, *ma petite*, and you will enjoy your tea, I am sure. A good conscience makes us enjoy our food well.'

When Mam'zelle, puzzled by the non-appearance of the girls back from their walk, sent Daphne down to see what had happened, the girl could have burst into tears when she saw the empty plates, the cake all gone, and the happy faces of the second-formers in the gym.

'You mean pigs!' she cried. 'You didn't go out after all! And you've had tea without me!'

'We couldn't disturb you at your extra French lesson,'

grinned Alicia. 'Dear Miss Parker quite agreed it would be a pity to spoil it for you, as you were so anxious to have it.'

Daphne glared at Gwendoline. '*You* might have come for me,' she said. 'You could easily have slipped off and fetched me!'

'The only person who tried to get you was Mary-Lou,' said Sally. 'She actually went up to Miss Parker and suggested that she should go and get you. Mary-Lou doesn't think that extra French is preferable to walks or games.'

Daphne looked at Mary-Lou and felt warm towards her. Not even Gwendoline, her friend, had tried to get her out of that awful French lesson to join the games. But Mary-Lou had. Mary-Lou had thought loyally of her.

'Thanks, Mary-Lou,' said Daphne, and turned a rather watery smile on her. 'I won't forget that. That was decent of you.'

From that time the selfish, boastful, untrustworthy Daphne was nice to Mary-Lou, not only because the smaller girl helped her so much with her French but because she really liked her and admired her. Perhaps never before had Daphne really liked anyone for themselves.

Mary-Lou, of course, was delighted. She had quite fallen under Daphne's spell, and was too simple to see the faults in the girl's character. She was very happy to be with her, and delighted to help her whenever she could. She did not even see that the help she gave almost amounted to making Daphne cheat, for many an evening she did practically the whole of Daphne's prep for her.

Gwendoline began to be jealous of Mary-Lou, for she sensed that Daphne was really beginning to like her very much. But Daphne always laughed when Gwendoline spoke to her about it.

'You *know* I'm only using her!' she said. 'Don't be a mutt, Gwen. You're my friend and I don't want anybody else. I've nothing whatever in common with Mary-Lou – She's a silly little simpleton, a stupid little mouse!'

It was a good thing that Mary-Lou did not hear these remarks, for she would have been shocked and hurt. She was very glad to feel that Daphne really did like her. She often lay in bed thinking of the girl's beautiful hair and lovely smile. She wished she was as charming as that. But she wasn't, and never would be.

Daphne did not forgive the others for being mean enough not to warn her, when they knew the walk was off. She was even a little cold to Gwendoline about it, and Gwendoline, fearful of losing her grand friend's liking, made haste to lick her boots again, listening to all Daphne's tales with most satisfactory attention.

Sally heard Daphne one evening. She was sitting near the curtain in the common-room and the two girls, Gwen and Daphne, did not see her.

'Didn't I ever tell you about the time my mother gave a party on board our yacht, and I sat next to the Prince at supper?' began Daphne.

'Were you allowed to sit up to supper?' said Gwendoline. 'And whatever did you find to say to a prince?'

'Oh, well – he seemed to admire my hair and talked to me awfully nicely,' said Daphne, beginning to embroider

66

her tale as usual. 'I stayed up till one o'clock that night. The yacht was lovely. It had little lights all over it, and people on land said it looked beautiful – like a ship in a fairy-tale.'

'What were you dressed in?' asked Gwendoline.

'Oh – a frilly frock with little pearls all over it and my pearl necklace. It's worth hundreds of pounds,' said Daphne.

Gwendoline gasped. 'Where is it?' she said.

'Oh, I'm not allowed to bring anything like that to school,' said Daphne. 'Mother's very strict about things of that sort, you know. I haven't any jewellery here – or grand dresses – or anything you haven't got.'

'No. I've noticed that – I think it's very sensible of your mother,' said Gwendoline.

Sally had got tired of all this grand talk. She slipped off the window-sill. 'It's a pity your mother didn't supply you with your own lacrosse stick, and another pair of shoes, and plenty of writing-paper,' she remarked. 'Then you wouldn't have to keep borrowing from everyone else! A little less yacht, and fewer cars – and more envelopes and a book of stamps would be better for you, Daphne!'

Daphne looked haughtily at Sally. 'Mind your own business!' she said. 'I was talking to Gwen.'

'It *is* my business!' persisted Sally. 'You are always borrowing from one or other of us – and you never pay back! As you're so rich, you ought to use some of your plentiful pocket-money to buy the things you lack!'

'Beast!' said Daphne, as Sally went out of the room. 'She's jealous of me, I suppose – just because *her* people aren't as well-off as mine!'

10 The two Mam'zelles

Half-term came and went. Sally and Darrell went out together with Darrell's parents and had a lovely time. To Gwendoline's disappointment, Daphne's parents did not visit her, so there was no chance of being asked out to meals with Daphne, or going off in a magnificent car.

'I wanted to see your mother,' said Gwendoline. 'She looks so lovely in her photo.'

On Daphne's dressing-table stood a photograph of a very beautiful woman, in a flowing evening gown, with gleaming jewels round her lovely neck. Everyone had admired it.

'You aren't much like your mother, all the same,' said Darrell, critically, to Daphne. 'She's got wide-set eyes – and yours are rather near together. And your nose isn't the same.'

'Everybody isn't always like their mother,' said Daphne. 'I take after my father's family, I suppose. I have an aunt who is very, very beautiful.'

'And I suppose you are considered to resemble her, Daphne?' said Jean, in her quiet, amused voice. 'What it is to have beautiful and distinguished relatives! I have a plain mother, who's the kindest darling on earth – and quite an ugly father – and all my aunts are as plain as I am! But I don't care a bit. They're jolly good fun, and I like the whole lot.'

Gwendoline asked Daphne if she would like to go out with her at half-term, and Daphne accepted graciously.

Mrs. Lacey, Gwendoline's mother, was very struck with the beautiful girl and her charming smile. As for Miss Winter, the governess, who always most faithfully came to see her darling Gwen every half-term, she could hardly take her eyes off her, which annoyed Gwendoline very much.

'*Such* a nice friend for you, dear,' said Mrs. Lacey to Gwendoline. 'Such beautiful manners! And how rich her people must be to own a yacht and all those cars. Wouldn't it be nice if you could go and stay with them?'

'Ssh, Mother,' said Gwendoline, afraid that Daphne would hear. But Daphne was far too busy charming poor Miss Winter. She played up to Gwendoline very well too, remarking on her friend's brilliance, her clever comments in class, and what a favourite she was with the teachers.

Mrs. Lacey listened with pride and pleasure. 'Well, you never told me these things in your letters, Gwen darling,' she said, fondly. 'You're too modest!'

Gwendoline felt a little embarrassed and began to hope that Daphne wouldn't lay it on too thickly – if she did, her mother would expect a wonderful report, and Gwendoline knew perfectly well there was no hope of that.

Belinda and Irene went out together, both forgetting their hats, and both returning without their gloves. They went with Belinda's parents, who appeared to be as bad as Belinda herself, for they lost the way when bringing the girls back to Malory Towers, and turned up over an hour late; much to Miss Parker's annoyance. She could not bear the time-table to be played about with. But neither Belinda nor Irene noticed her cold manner as they went noisily into the room to report their return to her.

Alicia and Betty had gone out together, of course, and had come back full of giggles. Apparently one of Alicia's brothers had been in the party, and had related with much gusto all the tricks that he and his class had been up to that term.

To everyone's surprise Jean had asked the bad-tempered, irritable Ellen to come out with her! Ellen had refused at first, rather ungraciously – and then had unexpectedly said she would. But it had not been a very pleasant outing, for Ellen had been rather silent and had not tried in any way to be pleasant to her hosts. She seemed sunk into herself, and Jean was sorry she had asked her.

'You might have been a bit more cheerful, Ellen,' she said, as they came into the school again. 'You hardly spoke and you didn't laugh once, even when my father made some quite good jokes!'

'Well, don't ask me out again then,' said Ellen, snappily, and turned away. Jean caught the gleam of tears in her eyes. Funny girl! So touchy that nobody could say a word to her without getting their head bitten off! Jean was beginning to be tired of her efforts to be nice to Ellen.

'Now we can look forward to Christmas!' said Darrell, with satisfaction. 'Half-term's over.'

'We've got those awful French plays to mug up now,' groaned Alicia. 'Whatever possessed the two Mam'zelles to think up such a horrible thing for the second form to do? Who wants to see us perform French plays?'

Each form had to produce some sort of entertainment at the end of the term. It was the lot of the second form to learn two French plays, one chosen by Mam'zelle Dupont, the other by Mam'zelle Rougier.

It was over the choosing of the girls to play the different characters in these plays that the two Mam'zelles almost came to blows.

In one play there was a Princess – the Princess True-Heart. In the other there was an angel – the Angel of Goodness. Mam'zelle Dupont wanted her favourite, Daphne, to play both parts. She pictured the pretty, golden-haired girl as the Princess – ah, how wonderful she would look! And as an angel! Truly Daphne was made for the part of an angel!

But Mam'zelle Rougier unfortunately had quite different ideas. 'What! You would choose that imbecile of a Daphne to play two good parts like that!' scoffed Mam'zelle Rougier. 'She could never learn half the words – and her pronunciation is AB–OM–IN–ABLE! You know it. I will not have that girl in a good part.'

'Ah, but she will look the parts to perfection!' cried Mam'zelle Dupont, sweeping her arms wide apart to emphasize her words. 'She looks a real Princess – and when she smiles, it is truly the smile of an angel.'

'Bah!' said Mam'zelle Rougier, rudely. 'She is one of your favourites, your little pets. Now Sally would do well in one of those parts – she would learn well and her pronunciation is good. Or Darrell. Or even Mary-Lou would be better than Daphne, for she at least speaks French as it should be spoken.'

'You are mad!' cried Mam'zelle Dupont. 'As if any of

those girls could play such parts as these. I insist on Daphne playing the parts.'

'Then I shall not have anything to do with the plays,' said Mam'zelle Rougier, stiffly. 'It is always a mistake to do as you do, Mamzelle Dupont, and have favourites – and when it comes to forcing them on me, it is finished!'

'I do not have favourites!' said Mam'zelle Dupont, untruthfully, tapping her foot on the ground. 'I like all the girls just the same.'

Mam'zelle Rougier snorted disbelievingly. 'Then you are the only one who thinks so,' she said. 'Good day, Mam'zelle. I cannot stand arguing here, talking nonsense about such girls as Daphne.'

She swung round and walked off stiffly, holding her thin bony body like a stick. Plump little Mam'zelle Dupont stared after her angrily. Favourites, indeed! How dared Mam'zelle say things like that to her? Never would she speak to Mam'zelle Rougier again. Never, never, never! She would leave Malory Towers. She would go back to her beloved France. She would write to the newspapers about it. Mam'zelle Dupont made a noise like the growling of a dog, and startled Miss Potts considerably as she came in at the door.

'Don't you feel well, Mam'zelle?' she said, rather alarmed at Mam'zelle's red face and glaring eyes.

'I do not feel at all well. I have been insulted,' said Mam'zelle Dupont. 'I am not to be allowed to choose the girls in my own plays. Mam'zelle Rougier objects to my choosing the pretty, charming Daphne for the Princess. She will not even allow me – me, Mam'zelle Dupont – to give her the part of the Angel of Goodness!'

'Well, I must say I agree with her,' said Miss Potts, sitting down and arranging her papers. 'Daphne always seems a double-faced little creature to me.'

'You too are in the plot against me!' said Mam'zelle, going all dramatic, and working herself up into a tearful rage. 'You too! Ah, these cold English people! Ah, these . . .'

Miss Potts was very glad indeed to hear a knock at the door at that moment. She didn't like dealing with Mam'zelle in these moods. Matron came in, smiling. 'Can I have a word with you, Mam'zelle?' she asked.

'No, you cannot,' said Mam'zelle, fiercely. 'I am upset. My heart it beats so – and so – and so. But I tell you this – I will choose what girl I wish for my plays. Ah-h-h-h!'

And, making a noise like a dog again, Mam'zelle walked angrily from the room, leaving Matron quite stupefied. 'Whatever is she talking about?' she asked Miss Potts.

'Oh, she's had some sort of upset with the other Mam'zelle,' said Miss Potts, beginning to add up marks. 'They get across one another at times, you know. But this appears to be more serious than usual. Well, they'll have to sort out their own tangles!'

Mam'zelle Dupont and Mam'zelle Rougier took it in turns to train the girls in the two French plays. Mam'zelle Dupont put Daphne into the two principal parts each time she took the play, much to the girl's gratification. But, equally promptly, Mam'zelle Rougier relegated her to a minor part the next day and put Sally and Darrell into the principal ones. It was most muddling.

Neither Mam'zelle would give way. The quarrel

appeared to be deadly and serious. They looked the other way when they met. They never spoke to one another. The girls thought it was a great joke, but on the whole they took Mam'zelle Dupont's part, for they liked her much the better of the two. They did not approve of her choice of Daphne for the principal parts, but that couldn't be helped.

Belinda, intrigued by the quarrel, did a masterly set of caricatures of Mam'zelle Rougier, taller and bonier than ever. She drew her with a dagger in her hand, stalking poor Mam'zelle Dupont. She drew her hiding behind a bush with a gun. She drew her pouring poison into a tea-cup to present to her enemy.

The girls giggled over the pictures. Alicia was very struck by them. A wicked idea came into her head.

'Belinda! Mam'zelle Dupont would adore these pictures! You know what a sense of humour she has. She ought to see them. Put them on her desk tomorrow afternoon, just before she takes French translation – and watch her face when she opens the book!'

'I bet we shan't have any French translation tomorrow afternoon once she sees the pictures!' giggled Betty, and the others agreed.

Belinda bound the pictures neatly into a book. She had put no name to them, but they were so cleverly drawn that anyone could see at once that they were meant to represent the two Mam'zelles. 'I'll pop it on the desk just before the afternoon class,' she said. 'And you can jolly well all of you do my prep for me tonight, to repay me for getting you off your French translation tomorrow!'

Alicia whispered something to Betty. Betty looked

74

startled and then grinned broadly. Alicia had just told her something interesting. 'It isn't Mam'zelle Dupont who's taking us tomorrow. It's Mam'zelle Rougier! Watch out for fireworks!'

11 A shock for the second form

The book of drawings was placed on the classroom desk in good time. The girls stood in their places, excited, waiting for Mam'zelle to come. How she would roar at the pictures! How she would enjoy the joke against her enemy, Mam'zelle Rougier!

Alicia was holding the door. It had been quite by chance that she had heard that the lesson was to be taken by Mam'zelle Rougier instead of Mam'zelle Dupont. She hugged herself secretly when she thought of the bomb-shell she had prepared. It would pay back Mam'zelle Rougier for many a sharp word she had given Alicia!

Quick footsteps came down the passage. The girls stiffened. Somebody came in at the door and went to the desk – but it wasn't the Mam'zelle they had been expect-ing. It was, of course, the other one. Mam'zelle Rougier seated herself and addressed the class.

'*Asseyez vous, s'il vous plaît*!'

Some of the girls forgot to sit down, so overcome with horror were they to think that Mam'zelle Rougier was sitting there with that book of caricatures right under her nose. Mam'zelle rapped on her desk.

'Are you deaf? Sit!'

They sat. Belinda stared beseechingly round. She caught Alicia's satisfied grin and felt angry. So Alicia had known that Mam'zelle Rougier was coming instead of Mam'zelle Dupont – and had used her as a cat's paw to play a very dangerous trick. Everyone knew what Mam'zelle Rougier's temper was like. She would probably go straight to the Head!

Belinda didn't know what to do. Darrell saw how alarmed she was, and did a bold thing. She got up and walked to Mam'zelle's desk, and put her hand on the book.

'I'm sorry this was left here by mistake, Mam'zelle,' she said, politely. She almost got away with it. But not quite. The girls stared breathlessly.

'Wait a moment,' said Mam'zelle Rougier. 'Books left on the desk must not be removed without permission. What is this book?'

'Oh – only a – a sketch-book,' said Darrell, desperately. Mam'zelle glanced round the silent class. Why were they all looking and listening so intently? There was something curious here.

She took up the book and opened it. Her glance fell on the picture of herself stalking Mam'zelle Dupont with a dagger. She stared at it incredulously. There she was in the picture, tall, thin, bony – positively evil-looking – and with a dagger too!

She turned over a page. What! Here she was again – with a gun. Ah, no, this was too much! She turned another page and another. Always she saw herself there, unkindly caricatured, pursuing poor Mam'zelle Dupont, who had been given a most amiable look, and was obviously the heroine, whilst she, Mam'zelle Rougier, was the villain!

'This is unbelievable!' said Mam'zelle, under her breath, almost forgetting Darrell, who stood petrified nearby, and all the other waiting girls. Belinda was very pale. What bad luck! Whatever would happen now? Oh, why had she been such an idiot as to let Alicia lead her into this silly trap – just to make Alicia and Betty enjoy seeing her well ticked-off.

Mam'zelle became aware of the girls again. She snapped at Darrell and made her jump. 'Go back to your place.'

Darrell fled thankfully. Mam'zelle looked round the class, raking them with cold, angry eyes.

'Who has done this? Who has committed the insult of placing this book beneath my eyes?'

Sally spoke up at once. 'We're all in it, Mam'zelle. But we didn't mean *you* to see the book. We meant it for Mam'zelle Dupont. We didn't know you had changed over lessons today.'

This was unfortunately the worst possible thing that Sally could have said. Mam'zelle shot to her feet at once, her eyes stony.

'What! You meant to give this to Mam'zelle Dupont! You meant her to laugh at me with you! Is that what she does behind my back? Ah, how glad I am to know how she behaves, this shameful Frenchwoman! She shall know of this! I go to Miss Grayling at once – this very minute!'

The class sat in horrified silence. It had not occurred to them that it might be insulting to Mam'zelle Rougier to show the book of comical drawings to Mam'zelle Dupont. Belinda felt faint.

'Mam'zelle! Don't go to Miss Grayling. I . . .'

But the class were not going to let Belinda take the blame. Even Alicia looked scared now. Many of the girls spoke at once, drowning poor Belinda's faint voice.

'Mam'zelle, we're sorry. Don't report us!'

But Mam'zelle, swept by a cold fury, was already departing out of the door. The girls looked at one another in real horror.

'Alicia – *you knew* Mam'zelle Rougier was coming this afternoon instead of Mam'zelle Dupont,' said Belinda. 'I saw you wink at Betty. You *knew*! And you used me to play one of your nasty tricks! I'd never have shown those pictures to Mam'zelle Rougier, and you know it.'

Alicia was truthful, whatever her faults were. She did not deny it. 'I didn't know she'd make such a fuss,' she said, rather feebly.

'Alicia, you're a beast!' said Darrell, feeling a hot flame working up inside her. 'You might have thought what serious trouble you'd get Belinda into. You, you . . .'

'Leave me to deal with this,' said Sally's quiet voice behind her. 'Don't get all worked up, Darrell. I'll deal with Alicia.'

'Oh, will you?' said Alicia, spitefully. 'Well, you won't. If you think you're going to tick me off, you're not,

Miss Head-of-the-Form, Good-Girl-of-the-School, Sally Hope.'

'Don't be silly,' said Sally, in disgust. 'I can't think what's come over you lately, Alicia. You are always trying to make things difficult for me. I'm going down to the Head myself, this very minute – and you're to come too, Belinda. We'll try to get things put straight before they go too far.'

'You'll put the whole blame on to me, of course!' said Alicia, scornfully. 'I know you! Get Belinda out of trouble and me into it!'

'I shan't say anything about you,' said Sally. 'I'm not a sneak. But I'd think a lot better of you if you came along with us, and explained your part in the affair!'

'I don't care what you think of me,' said Alicia, getting angry. 'I'm not going to tag along at your heels and say "Please, I did it!" You're not going to make me do anything I don't want to do!'

'I'm not going to try,' said Sally. 'Come on, Belinda, let's go before it's too late.'

Poor Belinda, looking frightened out of her life, went along the passage and down the stairs and out into the Court. They made their way to the Head Mistress's rooms.

'Oh, Sally – it's awful!' said Belinda, all her high spirits and light-heartedness gone. 'Mam'zelle was so fierce. And those pictures were rather beastly, some of them.'

When the girls knocked on the door of the Head Mistress's sitting-room, they heard voices inside. Miss Grayling was there, and Mam'zelle Rougier – and Miss Linnie the art-mistress. She had been called in to see if she could tell them who had done the clever and malicious drawings.

'Belinda Morris, of course!' she said, after a glance. 'There's no girl in the school as clever as she is at sketching. She'll be a first-class artist one of these days. My word – these *are* clever!'

'Clever!' snorted Mam'zelle. 'They are wicked, they are disrespectful, they are bad, bad, bad! I demand that you punish this girl, Miss Grayling. I demand that the whole class shall be severely punished too.'

Just at that moment Sally knocked at the door. 'Come in!' said Miss Grayling, and the two girls entered.

'Well?' said Miss Grayling. Sally swallowed hard. It was all very difficult – especially as Mam'zelle was glaring at her so fiercely.

'Miss Grayling,' she began, 'we're very, very sorry about this.'

'What is it to do with you?' asked Miss Grayling. 'I thought Belinda did the pictures?'

'Yes, I did,' said Belinda, in a low voice.

'But it was the whole class who wanted to put them on the desk – and let Mam'zelle Dupont see them,' said Sally. 'But – Mam'zelle Rougier came instead, and she saw them. I'm very sorry about it.'

'But why should you picture Mam'zelle Rougier pursuing her friend in such a murderous manner?' asked the Head, looking through the book. 'I don't see why that should interest or amuse Mam'zelle Dupont.'

There was a silence. Then Mam'zelle Rougier spoke stiffly. 'We are not friends, Mam'zelle Dupont and I.'

And before Miss Grayling could stop her, Mam'zelle

had poured out her grievance over the plays. Miss Grayling listened gravely. Then she turned to the girls.

'Then do I understand that one day the chief characters are played by Sally and Darrell, and the next day by Daphne?' she asked.

Sally said yes, that was what had happened. Mam'zelle Rougier suddenly looked rather ashamed. It occurred to her that she and Mam'zelle Dupont had been very silly, and had allowed their private quarrel to muddle up the play and make things awkward for the girls.

She wished she had thought twice about taking the book down to the Head. No wonder the girls had put the quarrel into those stupid drawings – but why did they make her the villain and Mam'zelle Dupont the heroine? Ah, that was not nice!

'You didn't know, then, that Mam'zelle Rougier was going to take the class instead of Mam'zelle Dupont?' said the Head, suddenly. Sally hesitated a fraction of a second. Alicia had known – and Betty too. But she, Sally, hadn't known, nor had any of the others.

'I didn't know that, of course, Miss Grayling,' she said.

'Did anyone know?' persisted the Head. Sally did not know how to answer. She did not want to tell tales, but she could not very well say nothing. Belinda broke in.

'Yes, someone knew – and that someone used me for a cat's paw. I'd never, never have shown those drawings to Mam'zelle Rougier. I won't tell who it was – but do believe me when I say I wouldn't have hurt Mam'zelle Rougier's feelings for anything. It was just a joke.'

'Yes, I see that,' said Miss Grayling. 'An unfortunate

82

joke, of course, but still a joke. A joke that was played on the wrong person and caused anger and distress. As I see it, quite a lot of people are to blame in this.' She glanced at Mam'zelle Rougier, who grew rather red. 'There was a quarrel, it seems, to start with. Without that, possibly all this would not have occurred. You two girls may go now. I will discuss with Mam'zelle what punishment is fitting for you all.'

In silence Belinda and Sally went out of the door. Miss Linnie came with them. Mam'zelle Rougier was left behind, as Miss Grayling had made her a sign to stop.

'Belinda, you're an idiot,' said Miss Linnie.

'I'll never draw anyone again!' said Belinda, dismally.

'Oh, yes you will!' said Miss Linnie. 'But you'll probably draw kinder pictures in future. Don't be too clever, Belinda – it always lands you into trouble sooner or later!'

12 Mam'zelle Dupont puts things right

Upstairs something was happening. Mam'zelle Dupont had come past the door of the second form, and had found it open. On looking in, she had found, to her surprise, that Mam'zelle Rougier had apparently deserted her form and left the girls alone. More surprising still, the girls were sitting as quiet as mice – and what long faces!

'What is the matter, *mes petites*?' cried Mam'zelle, her little beady eyes ranging over the silent class. 'What has happened?'

Mary-Lou, thoroughly upset by everything, gave an unexpected sob. Mam'zelle turned to her. Mary-Lou was one of her pets, for Mary-Lou could chatter French perfectly.

'What is wrong, then! Tell me! Am I not your friend! What is this that has happened?'

'Oh, Mam'zelle – an awful thing has happened!' burst out Mary-Lou. 'Belinda did some pictures of you and Mam'zelle Rougier. Nice ones of you but awful ones of Mam'zelle Rougier – and we didn't know Mam'zelle was coming instead of you this afternoon – and we put the book on the desk for *you* to see, and . . . and . . .'

'Ah! Mam'zelle Rougier, she saw them instead, and she has gone blue in the face, and she has taken Belinda and poor Sally to Miss Grayling!' cried Mam'zelle. 'Ah, this bad-tempered woman! She cannot see a joke. I, I myself, will go to see Miss Grayling. I will tell her one, two, three things about Mam'zelle Rougier! Ah-h-h!'

And off went Mam'zelle Dupont, scuttling along on her high heels like a harassed rabbit. The girls looked at one another. What an afternoon!

Mam'zelle did not meet Belinda and Sally, for they went different ways. Just at the moment that she knocked at Miss Grayling's door, Sally and Belinda walked into the classroom, looking rather gloomy. They reported what had happened.

'So you did split on me after all,' said Alicia, in disgust.

'We didn't even mention your name,' said Belinda. 'So you needn't be afraid, Alicia.'

'I'm not afraid!' said Alicia. But she was. She hadn't been in Miss Grayling's good books lately and she knew it. She didn't want to be hauled over the coals for this now. But she didn't like the girls' scornful glances.

'Mam'zelle Dupont's gone off to join the merry family now,' said Darrell. 'I wonder what is happening.'

Mam'zelle Dupont had swept into the Head's sitting-room, startling both Miss Grayling and Mam'zelle Rougier. Miss Grayling was just getting an account of the quarrel between the two French mistresses from a rather shame-faced Mam'zelle Rougier, when the other Mam'zelle swept in.

She saw the book of drawings at once and picked them up. She examined them. 'Ah, *là, là*! This Belinda is a genius! Ha ha! – look at me here, Miss Grayling – did you ever see such a plump rabbit as I look? And oh, Mam'zelle Rougier, what are you doing with that dagger? It is marvellous, wonderful! But see here! I am to be poisoned!'

Mam'zelle Dupont went off into peals of laughter. She wiped the tears from her eyes. 'You do not think it is funny?' she said in astonishment to the other mistresses. 'But look – look – here I am to be shot with this gun. As if my good friend Mam'zelle Rougier would do such a thing to me! Ah, we quarrel sometimes, she and I, but it matters nothing! We are two Frenchwomen together, *n'est-ce pas*, Mam'zelle Rougier, and we have much to put up with from these bad English girls!'

Mam'zelle Rougier began to look a little less frigid. Miss Grayling looked at one or two of the pictures and allowed herself to smile. 'This one is really very funny, Mam'zelle Dupont,' she said. 'And this one, too. Of course, the whole thing is most disrespectful, and I want you both to say what punishment we must give the class – and especially, of course, Belinda.'

There was a silence. 'I feel,' began Mam'zelle Rougier, at last, 'I feel, Miss Grayling, that perhaps Mam'zelle Dupont and I are a little to blame for all this – our stupid quarrel, you know – naturally it intrigues the girls – and . . .'

'Ah, yes, you are right!' cried Mam'zelle Dupont, fervently. 'You are quite, quite right, my friend. It is we who are to blame. Miss Grayling – we demand no punishment for the bad, bad girls! We will forgive them.'

Mam'zelle Rougier looked a little taken aback. Why should Mam'zelle Dupont forgive them? They hadn't drawn *her* unkindly! But Mam'zelle Dupont was rushing on in her headlong way.

'These pictures, they are more funny than bad! It is a tease, a joke, is it not? We do not mind! It was our stupid quarrel that started it. But now, now we are friends, are we not, Mam'zelle Rougier?'

Mam'zelle Rougier could not say no to that. Swept away in spite of herself, she nodded. Mam'zelle Dupont gave her two sudden and exuberant kisses, one on each cheek. Miss Grayling was much amused.

'That Belinda!' said Mam'zelle Dupont, looking at the drawings again. 'Ah, what a clever child. One day, maybe, Miss Grayling, we shall be proud of these

86

drawings! When Belinda is famous, Mam'zelle Rougier and I, we shall look together with pride on these pictures, and we shall say, "Ah, the little Belinda did these for us when she was in our class!" '

Mam'zelle Rougier said nothing to this. She was feeling that she had been made to do all kinds of things she hadn't meant to do. But she couldn't go back on what she had said now. That was certain.

'Well, perhaps you would go back to your classes now,' suggested Miss Grayling. 'And you will tell the girls, and set their minds at rest? Belinda must apologize, of course. But I think you'll find she will do that without any prompting.'

The two Mam'zelle departed, arm-in-arm. The girls they met stared at them in surprise, for everyone knew that the two had been bitter enemies for the last week or so. They went up to the second form, who stood in silence, glad to see Mam'zelle Dupont looking so cheerful, and the other Mam'zelle not quite so sour as usual.

Mam'zelle Dupont set their minds at rest. 'You have been bad girls. Very bad girls. Belinda, you let your pencil run away with you. I am shocked!'

She didn't look shocked. Her beady black eyes twinkled. Belinda stood up.

'I want to apologize,' she said, rather shakily, 'to both of you.'

Mam'zelle Rougier didn't see any necessity for Belinda to apologize to Mam'zelle Dupont, but she didn't say so. She accepted the apology as graciously as she could.

'And now for punishment,' said Mam'zelle Dupont, in

a stern voice, but still with twinkling eyes, 'for punishment you will pay better attention to your French lessons than you have ever done before. You will learn well, you will translate marvellously, you will be my best pupils. Is that not so?'

'Oh, *yes*, Mam'zelle,' promised the girls fervently, and, for the time being at any rate, even Gwendoline and Daphne meant it! Mam'zelle Rougier went. Mam'zelle Dupont took over the five remaining minutes of the lesson.

'Please,' said Darrell, at the end, 'Mam'zelle, will you tell us who *is* to take the chief parts in the French plays we're doing? It's so muddling not knowing. Perhaps you and Mam'zelle Rougier have settled it now.'

'We have not,' said Mam'zelle Dupont, 'but I, I am generous today. I will let the poor Mam'zelle Rougier have her way, to make up to her for the shock you have given her this morning. I will not take Daphne for the chief parts. You, Darrell and Sally, shall have them. That will please Mam'zelle Rougier and put her into such a good mood that she will smile on you all!'

Daphne was not too pleased about this. She looked at Mam'zelle, rather hurt. All the same, it was a good thing, she thought, because how she was EVER going to learn all that French talk in the play she really didn't know? Perhaps it would be just as well if she didn't have the chief parts, after all. She would look hurt, but be very sweet and generous about it!

So, looking rather stricken, she spoke to Mam'zelle. 'It's just as you like, Mam'zelle. I *had* been looking forward to swotting up my parts for you – but I hope I'm generous enough to give them up to others without a fuss!'

'The kind girl!' said Mam'zelle, beaming. 'I will make it up to you, Daphne. You shall come to me and we will read together a French book I loved when I was a girl. Ah, that will be a treat for both of us!'

The class wanted to laugh when they saw Daphne's horrified face. Read a French book with Mam'zelle! How dreadful. She would have to get out of that somehow.

The affair of the drawings had three results. Alicia was sulky, because she felt she had come out very badly in the matter, and she knew that Sally and Darrell and some of the others didn't think very much of her because of it. The two Mam'zelles were firm friends now, instead of enemies. And Daphne was now given a very minor part indeed in the plays, where she would not appear as someone beautiful, but only as an old man in a hood. She was very much disgusted.

'Especially as I've written and told my people all about my fine parts,' she complained. 'It's a shame.'

'Yes, it is,' said Gwendoline. 'Never mind, Daphne – you won't have to do all that swotting now!'

Jean came up with a box at that moment. She jingled it under their noses. 'Have you got your games sub, you two? We're collecting it today. Two pounds each.'

'Here's mine,' said Gwendoline, getting out her purse.

'Yours, please, Daphne,' said Jean. Daphne took out her purse. 'Blow!' she said. 'I thought I had five pounds, but there's only fifty pence. Oh, yes – I had to buy a birthday present for my governess last week. Gwen, lend me the money till I get some from home, will you?'

'She lent you two pounds last week,' said Jean, jingling the box again. 'I bet you didn't pay her back! And you borrowed fifty pence off me for church collection, let me tell you. Why don't you keep a little book showing your debts?'

'What do little sums like that matter?' said Daphne, annoyed. 'I'll be getting pounds and pounds on my birthday soon. Anyway, I can pay back this week. My uncle is sending me ten pounds.'

'Well, I'll lend you two pounds till then,' said Gwendoline, and put four pounds into the box. Jean turned to Darrell and collected her money. She went to Ellen and jingled the box under her nose.

'Two pounds, please, Ellen.'

'Don't do that under my nose!' said Ellen, jumping. 'What is it you want? Two pounds? Well, I haven't got it on me just now. I'll give it to you later.'

'You said that last time,' said Jean, who was a most persistent person when it came to collecting money. 'Go on – get it, Ellen, and then the collection will be finished.'

'I'm working,' said Ellen annoyed. 'Take the thing away. I'll give you the money soon.'

Jean went off, also annoyed. Daphne spoke in a low voice to Gwendoline. 'I bet she hasn't got the two pounds to give! She won a scholarship here, but I don't believe her people can really afford to keep her at a school like this!'

Ellen didn't quite hear what was said but she knew it was something nasty, by Daphne's sneering tone. She flung down her book. 'Can't *any*body work in this place!'

90

she said. 'Stop your whispering, Daphne, and take that smile off your silly face!'

13 Poor Ellen!

'Really!' said Daphne, as Ellen walked out of the room and banged the door. 'What awful manners that girl's got! What's the matter with her?'

Nobody knew. Nobody guessed that Ellen was getting more and more worried about her work. She knew that the end of term tests were coming along, and she wanted to come out well in them. She must! So she was working hard every minute, and she had begun to feel at last that she would be able to face the tests and do well.

But that evening she did not feel very well. Her throat hurt her. Her eyes hurt her, especially when she moved them about. She coughed.

Surely she wasn't going to be ill! That would put her terribly behind in her work. It would never do. So Ellen dosed herself with cough lozenges, and gargled secretly in the bathroom, hoping that Matron would not notice anything wrong.

Her eyes were too bright that evening. Her usually pale cheeks were red. She coughed in prep. Miss Potts, who was taking prep, looked at her.

'Do you feel all right, Ellen?' she asked.

'Oh, quite all right, Miss Potts,' said Ellen, untruthfully, and bent her head over her book. She coughed again.

'I don't like that cough,' said Miss Potts. 'I think perhaps you had better go to . . .'

'Oh, Miss Potts, it's only a tickle in my throat,' said Ellen, desperately. 'Perhaps I'd better get a drink of water.'

'Well, go then,' said Miss Potts, still not quite satisfied. So Ellen went. She leaned her hot head against the cool wall of the cloakroom and wished miserably that she had someone she could confide in. But her snappiness and irritability had put everyone against her – even Jean. Jean had tried to be nice – and Ellen hadn't even bothered to go and get the games subscription for her.

I don't know what's come over me lately, thought the girl. I used not to be like this, surely. I had plenty of friends at my other school. I wish I'd never left there. I wish I'd never won a scholarship!

She must go back. Her throat still hurt her and she slipped a lozenge into her mouth. Then she went back to the classroom, trying to walk firmly, though her legs felt rather wobbly.

She had a high temperature and should have been tucked up in bed. But she wasn't going to give in. She must do her work. She mustn't get behind. She must do well in the tests, whatever happened.

She tried to learn some French poetry, but it buzzed round and round in her head. She began to cough again.

'Oh, shut up,' said Alicia, in a whisper. 'You're putting it on to get Potty's sympathy!'

That was so like Alicia! She didn't like people who coughed or sniffed or groaned. She had no sympathy to spare for those who needed it. She was a healthy, strong, clever girl, who had never been ill in her life, and she scorned stupid people, or those who were delicate and ailing, or in trouble. She was hard, and it didn't seem as if she was getting any kinder. Darrell often wondered how she could so badly have wanted Alicia to be her friend when she had first come to Malory Towers!

Ellen looked at Alicia with dislike. 'I can't help it,' she said. 'I'm not putting it on.' She sneezed and Alicia gave an exclamation of disgust.

'Don't! Go to bed if you're as bad as all that!'

'Silence!' said Miss Potts, annoyed. Alicia said no more. Ellen sighed and tried to concentrate on her book again. But she couldn't. She was glad when the bell went and she could get up and go out into the cooler air. She was hot and yet she shivered. Oh, blow, she certainly was in for a cold. Perhaps it would be better tomorrow.

She tried to stuff some food down her throat at suppertime, in case Miss Parker noticed she wasn't eating anything. But Miss Parker did not often take any notice of Ellen. She was usually a quiet girl, with a name for bad temper, and Miss Parker was not at all interested in her, though sometimes surprised that her work was not better.

It was Sally who noticed that Ellen seemed ill that night. She heard her quick, rather hoarse breathing and looked at her in concern. She remembered how Ellen had coughed in prep. Poor Ellen – was she feeling simply awful, and not wanting to make a fuss?

Sally was both sensible and kind. She went to Ellen and took her hot hands. 'Ellen! You're not well! Let me go with you to Matron, silly!'

The little act of kindness made the tears start to Ellen's eyes. But she shook her head impatiently.

'I'm all right. Leave me alone! Just got a headache, that's all.'

'Poor old Ellen,' said Sally. 'You've got more than a headache. Come along to Matron. You ought to be in bed!'

But Ellen wouldn't go. It was not until Jean came up and sympathized with her that she broke down and confessed that yes, she really did feel awful, but she couldn't possibly go to bed with all that work to do before the tests! 'I must do well, you see,' she kept saying. 'I must.' The tears ran down her cheeks as she spoke, and she suddenly shivered.

'You won't do any good by keeping up when you should be in bed,' said Jean. 'Come along. I'll keep you well posted in what we do in lessons, I promise you! I'll make notes for you and everything!'

'Oh, will you?' said poor Ellen, coughing. 'All right then. If you'll help me to catch up, I'll go and see Matron now. Perhaps just one day in bed will put me right.'

But one day was certainly not going to put Ellen right! She was very ill and Matron put her to bed in the san at once. Ellen was so thankful to be there that she couldn't help crying. She was ashamed of herself, but she couldn't stop the tears.

'Now don't you worry,' said Matron, kindly. 'You should have been in bed days ago by the look of you! Silly child! Now you just lie still and enjoy a week in bed.'

A week! Ellen started up in horror. She couldn't

possibly miss a week's work. She stared at Matron in dismay. Matron pushed her back.

'Don't look so horrified. You'll enjoy it. And as soon as you feel like it, and your cold is not infectious, you can choose a visitor.'

'Poor Ellen's really ill,' said Jean, as she went back to the others. 'I don't know what her temperature is, but I saw Matron's face when she took it, and it must be pretty high.'

'She coughed like anything in prep tonight,' said Sally. 'I felt sorry for her.'

'Well, Alicia didn't,' said Gwen, maliciously. 'She told her to shut up! Dear, kind Alicia!'

Alicia glared. She was always making sharp remarks about Gwen – but this time Gwen had got one back at *her* – and Alicia didn't much like it.

'Oh, we all know that Alicia can't bear to give a little sympathy out,' said Darrell, unable to stop herself. She had felt annoyed with Alicia lately, because she had been so offhand with Sally. Also she had thought that Alicia should certainly have owned up that it was she who had known Mam'zelle Rougier was going to take the lesson instead of Mam'zelle Dupont. She had made Belinda get into a row, when she could have prevented it.

Alicia, too, was ashamed of this now. But it was too late to do anything about it. There was no point in owning up now that the matter was closed. But she kept kicking herself for not doing so at the right time. She had been too obstinate.

She was sorry too that she had been hard on Ellen that evening – but how could she know she was really ill? She hadn't any time for that silly Ellen, always snapping and snarling at everyone! Let her be ill! A good thing if she *was* away from the class for a while. *She* wouldn't miss her!

Ellen felt very ill for four days, then she felt a little better. Her temperature went down, and she began to take a little more interest in things. But alas! Her old worry came back immediately she was well enough to think clearly!

Those tests! She knew that on the result of the tests depended her place in form. And it was very important that she should be top or nearly top. Her father and mother were so very proud that she had won the scholarship to such a fine school. They were not well-off, but they had told Ellen they would do anything they could to keep her at Malory Towers, now that she had won the right to be there by her own hard work.

The uniform had been so expensive. Even the train fare was expensive. It was a good thing she had been able to get a lift down in somebody's car. Mother had bought her a new trunk and a new suitcase. More expense. Oh, dear – was it really a good thing to win a scholarship to a school like Malory Towers if you had to count your pennies? Perhaps it wasn't.

And all the time she was losing her school work, and would do badly her first term. Her parents would be bitterly disappointed.

So Ellen worried and worried. The matron and the nurse couldn't think why she did not throw off her illness as quickly as she should. Every day she begged to be allowed to get up, but Matron shook her head. 'No, you can't, dear. You're not quite right yet. But would you like a visitor now? You can have one if you like.'

'Oh, yes. I'd like Jean, please,' said Ellen at once. Jean had promised to take notes for her. Jean would tell her all about the lessons she had missed. Jean was dependable and reliable.

So Jean came to see her, bringing a pot of honey. But it was not honey that Ellen wanted. She hardly even glanced at it.

'Did you bring the notes you said you would make for me?' she asked, eagerly. 'Oh, Jean – didn't you?'

'Good gracious me – what do you want notes of lessons for already?' demanded Jean, in astonishment. 'You're not even up!'

'Oh, I do, I do,' said Ellen. 'You promised, Jean. Well, bring them next time. You tell me all the lessons you've had now.'

Jean screwed up her eyes and tried to remember. She thought Ellen odd to want to talk about lessons instead of games or fun. She began to tell Ellen.

'Well, in maths we did those new sums again. I can bring you some to show you. And in French we learned that long piece of poetry on page sixty-four. I can recite some of it if you like. And for geography we learned . . .'

Matron bustled up. 'Jean! Ellen mustn't hear a word about lessons yet! She mustn't start worrying her head about work. She couldn't help missing it, and Miss Parker and Mam'zelle will quite understand that she will be a bit behind when she comes back.'

Ellen stared at her in consternation. 'But, Matron! I *must* know it all. I must! Oh, do let Jean tell me. And she's going to bring me some lesson notes she's made for me too.'

'Well, she certainly mustn't. I forbid it,' said Matron. So that was that. Ellen took no more interest in Jean's conversation. She lay back, desperate. She'd be near the bottom now! How unlucky she was!

14 Ellen has a bad idea

Nobody missed Ellen very much. She hadn't any of Darrell's high spirits or friendliness, none of Alicia's mischief or fun, she hadn't even the shyness and timidity of Mary-Lou, that made her missed when she wasn't there.

'You don't much notice Mary-Lou when she's there under your nose – but you do miss her when she's not,' said Darrell once. And that was true.

Darrell was missing Mary-Lou quite a lot these days, for Mary-Lou was attaching herself firmly to Daphne. Nobody could quite understand it. Nobody believed that Daphne wanted Mary-Lou's friendship – she only wanted her help in French. Even when Darrell pointed out that it was almost cheating for Mary-Lou to do such a lot for her, she would hardly listen.

'I can't do much to help anybody,' said Mary-Lou. 'It's only in French that I'm really good – and it's so nice to help somebody who wants it. And besides – Daphne does really like me, Darrell!'

'Well, so do I like you, and so does Sally,' said Darrell, really exasperated to think that Mary-Lou should attach herself to such a double-faced person as Daphne.

'Yes, I know. But you only put up with me out of the kindness of your heart!' said Mary-Lou. 'You've got Sally. You let me tag along behind you like a nice puppy – but you don't really want me, and I couldn't possibly help you in any way. But I *can* help Daphne – and though I know you think she's only using me for her French, she's not.'

Darrell was certain that Daphne only put up with Mary-Lou because of the French – but she wasn't quite right. Daphne was very fond of Mary-Lou now. She couldn't quite think why, because it wasn't like her to be fond of anyone – but Mary-Lou was so unobtrusive, so shy, so willing to help in any way. She's like a pet mouse, that you want to protect and take care of! thought Daphne. You can't help liking a mouse.

She poured out her tales of wealth to Mary-Lou, and Mary-Lou listened in the most gratifying manner. The younger girl was proud that someone as grand as Daphne should bother to notice her and talk to her and tell her things.

Ellen was away from school eleven days and had worried terribly the last six or seven because Jean had not been allowed to bring her lesson-notes or to tell her about the lessons. Now she came back, pale, a little thinner, with an obstinate look in her eyes. She was going to catch up somehow! If she had to get up at six in the morning, and learn her lessons under the sheets by means of a torch she would!

She asked Miss Parker if she would be kind enough to give her extra coaching in what she had missed. Miss Parker refused in a kindly manner.

'No, Ellen. You're not up even to your ordinary work at the moment, let alone taking extra coaching. I shan't expect much from you, nor will anyone else. So don't worry.'

Ellen went to Mam'zelle Dupont and even to Mam'zelle Rougier. 'I do so want to know what I've missed so that I can make it up,' she said. 'Could you give me a little extra coaching?'

But neither of the Mam'zelles would. 'You are not yet quite strong, *mon enfant*!' said Mam'zelle Dupont, kindly. 'No one will expect you to do brilliantly now this term. Take things more easily.'

So poor Ellen was quite in despair. Nobody would help her! They all seemed to be in a league against her – Matron, Doctor, Miss Parker, the two Mam'zelles.

And in ten days' time the tests began! Ellen usually liked exams, but she was dreading these. She couldn't think how it was that the girls joked about them so light-heartedly.

Then an idea came to her – a bad idea, that at first she put away from her mind at once. But it came back again and again, whispering itself into her mind so that she had to listen to it.

If you could perhaps see the test-papers before they were given out! If you could read the questions and know what you were going to be asked!

Ellen had never cheated in her life. She had never needed to for she had good brains and she knew how to work hard. People didn't cheat if they could do as well or better without cheating! Ah, but when you couldn't, when something had gone wrong, and you didn't know your work – would you cheat then if it was the only way to gain a good place?

It is not often that a test like that comes to a person with good brains, who has always scorned cheating – but now it came to Ellen. It is easy not to cheat if you don't need to. Is it easy not to cheat if you *do* need to? When that test comes, you will know your character for what it is, weak or strong, crooked or upright.

Ellen could no longer push the thought out of her mind. It was always there. Then one day she was in Miss Parker's room and saw what she thought was a test-paper on her desk. Miss Parker was not in the room. It needed only a moment to slip round and look at the paper.

Ellen read swiftly down the questions. How easy they were! Then, with a shock she saw that they were questions set for the first form, not the second. Her heart sank.

Before she could look for the second-form questions and see if they were there she heard Miss Parker's footsteps and slipped round to the other side of the desk. She must never let anyone guess that she was thinking of doing such a dreadful thing.

Ellen was always slipping into Miss Parker's room, or Miss Potts' room after that. She chose times when she knew they would not be there. She even went through Miss Parker's desk in the second-form room one morning after school hoping to find something there in the way of test questions.

Alicia found her there and looked surprised. 'What *are* you doing?' she said. 'You know we're not supposed to go to that desk. Really, Ellen!'

'I've lost my fountain-pen,' mumbled Ellen. 'I wondered if perhaps Miss Parker had . . .'

'Well, even if she *had* got it, you shouldn't go sneaking in her desk,' said Alicia, scornfully.

Then another time Darrell found her in Miss Potts' room, standing at Mam'zelle's empty desk, running her fingers through the papers there. She stared in surprise.

'Oh – er – Mam'zelle sent me here to find a book for her,' said Ellen, and was shocked at herself. She had always heard that one sin leads to another, and she was finding out that this was true. She was trying to cheat – and that made her tell untruths. What next would it be?

'Well, I must say Ellen isn't much improved by being away for nearly a fortnight,' said Betty, one evening in the common-room, when Ellen had snapped someone's head off, and gone out sulkily. 'She's just as snappy as ever – and she doesn't look a bit well yet.'

'Bad temper's her trouble,' said Alicia. 'I'm fed up with her. Always frowning and sighing and looking miserable!'

Gwendoline came in, looking bothered. 'Anyone seen my purse? I'm sure I put it into my desk, and now it's gone. And I put a five pound note in it only this morning, because I wanted to go out and buy something! Now I can't!'

'I'll help you to look for it,' said Daphne obligingly,

and got up. 'I bet it's still in your desk somewhere!'

But it wasn't. It was most annoying. Gwendoline screwed up her forehead and tried in vain to think if she had put it anywhere else.

'I'm sure I didn't,' she said at last. 'Oh, how sickening it is. Can you lend me some money, Daphne?'

'Yes. I've got my purse in my pocket,' said Daphne. 'Anyway I owe you some. I meant to have paid you before. I got some money yesterday from my uncle.'

She felt in her pocket and then looked up, a dismayed expression on her face. 'It's gone! There's a hole in my pocket! Blow! Wherever can I have dropped it?'

'Well, I must say you're a pretty pair!' said Alicia. 'Both of you losing your purses – just when they are full of money too! You're as bad as Irene or Belinda!'

Belinda had lost a two pound coin only the day before, and had crawled all over the form-room floor looking for it, much to Mam'zelle's amazement. She hadn't found it and had demanded her games subscription back from Jean. She hadn't got it, however, for Jean maintained that once the money had gone into her box, it was no longer the giver's – it belonged to the Games' secretary, or the school, or whatever fund it was meant for.

The two purses didn't turn up. It was annoying and rather mysterious. *Two* purses – full of money. Gwendoline looked at Daphne and lowered her voice. 'You don't think somebody's taken them, do you? Surely there couldn't be anyone in our form that would do a thing like that!'

Alicia was very curious about the purses. Into her mind slid the memory of seeing Ellen going through the

mistress's desk in the second-form room. Why should she do that? She had said she had lost her fountain-pen – but she hadn't, because Alicia had seen her using it at the very next lesson. Well, then . . .

Alicia determined to keep an eye on Ellen. If she was doing anything dishonest or underhand it ought to be reported to Sally. It was tiresome to think that Sally would have the right to hear about it and settle whether or not it should go before Miss Parker. Alicia felt the usual stab of jealousy when she thought of Sally as head-girl.

Ellen didn't know that Alicia was keeping an eye on her, but she did know that she was suddenly finding it very difficult to be alone, or to go into either Miss Parker's room, or Miss Potts' room, or even the form-room when nobody else was there. Alicia always seemed to pop up and say:

'Hallo, Ellen! Looking for somebody? Can I help you?'

Daphne borrowed as usual from somebody, but Gwendoline didn't. Gwedoline had been taught not to borrow, and she had written to ask her people to send her some more money to get on with. Daphne borrowed some from Mary-Lou and then offered half of it to Gwendoline.

'Oh *no*,' said Gwendoline, a little shocked. 'You can't lend other people's money to me, Daphne! I know you borrowed that from Mary-Lou. Why don't you do as I'm doing and wait till you get some more from your people? That's the worst of being as rich as you are – I suppose you just simply don't understand the value of money!'

Daphne looked a little surprised, for this was the first

time she had ever had any kind of criticism, even slight, from her faithful Gwendoline. Then she slipped her arm through her friend's.

'I expect you're right!' she said. 'I've always had as much money as I wanted – I don't really know the value of it. It's the way I've been brought up. Don't be cross, Gwen.'

'I don't know what would happen to you if you were ever in real need of money!' said Gwendoline. 'You *would* be miserable without your yacht and your cars and your staff and your beautiful house! How I wish I could see them all!'

But Daphne did not say, as Gwen always hoped she would, 'Well, come and stay with me for the holidays!' It rather looked as if Gwendoline would not be seeing her grand friend during the Christmas holidays, or attending parties and pantomimes with her. It rather looked as if she would have to put up with her own home and adoring mother and worshipping governess!

15 A dreadful evening

It was the day before the tests were to begin. Some of the girls were swotting up hard, feeling rather guilty because they hadn't paid as much attention to their work as they ought to have done. Betty Hill was poring over her books.

So was Gwendoline. And, as usual, poor Ellen had her nose between the pages of a book, trying to cram into a short time what could only be learned slowly and in peace.

Miss Parker was quite worried about Ellen. The girl gave her a strained attention in class, and yet her work was only fair. It wasn't for lack of trying, Miss Parker knew. She supposed it must be that Ellen was not very fit after her illness.

Ellen knew that the test-papers were ready. She had heard Miss Parker talking about them. As for Mam'zelle, in her usual tantalizing manner she had shaken her test-paper in front of her class, and cried 'Ah, you would like to know what I have set you, would you not! You would like to know what are these difficult questions! Now the first one is . . .'

But she never did say what the first one was, and the class laughed. Anyway, Mam'zelle Dupont was never so strict over tests as Mam'zelle Rougier, who set the most difficult questions and expected them to be answered perfectly – and then groaned and grumbled because nearly all the girls failed to get high marks!

It was Ellen's last chance that day to try to see the papers. If only that irritating Alicia wouldn't always keep hanging around! The thought occurred to Ellen that Alicia might be spying on her – but she dismissed it at once. Why should she? Nobody in the world save Ellen herself knew that she wanted to see the test-papers.

She hung about in the passage outside Miss Parker's room for a long time that evening. But there was never any chance of going in without being seen. Somebody always seemed to be going by. It was astonishing how many girls went this way and that way past Miss Parker's door.

Then, most annoyingly, the only time that the passage was really empty was when Miss Parker herself was in the room. She was there with Miss Potts. Ellen could quite well hear what they were saying.

She bent down by the door as if she was re-tying her shoe-lace.

'The second form haven't done too badly this term,' she heard Miss Parker say to Miss Potts. 'They seem to have benefited by the year they spent with you! Most of them can use their brains, which is something!'

'Well, I hope they do well in the tests,' said Miss Potts. 'I always take an interest in their first tests when they go up to the second form for the first time. Having had the girls for three or four terms I can't lose my interest in them quickly. I suppose Alicia or Irene or Darrell will be top. They've all got good brains.'

'Have a look at the questions,' said Miss Parker, and Ellen actually heard the rustling of the test-papers being handed over to Miss Potts. How she longed to see them!

There was a silence as Miss Potts read them. 'Yes. A bit stiff, one or two of them – but if the girls have paid attention, they ought to do them all quite well. What about the French papers?'

'Mam'zelle's got them in her room,' said Miss Parker. 'I'll take these along to her and give them to her. She takes the second form first thing tomorrow and can take the papers there with her.'

Ellen's heart leaped. Now she knew where the papers

would be that night! In Mam'zelle's room. And that was not very far from the dormy. Could she – dare she – get up in the night and go and peep at them?

A girl came round the corner and almost knocked Ellen over. It was Alicia.

'Gracious, it's you, Ellen! You were lounging about here when I came up – and now I come down and you're still here! What on earth are you doing?'

'It's no business of yours!' said Ellen, and walked off. She went to the common-room and sat down. She had to work things out. Dare she creep out in the middle of the night and hunt for the papers? It was a very, very wrong thing to do. But oh, if only she had been well all the term, and had been able to work and use her brains properly, she could easily have been top or near the top. It wasn't her fault that she would be near the bottom.

So she sat and reasoned with herself, trying to persuade herself that what she was doing wasn't really so bad as it looked. She was doing it to save her parents from being so disappointed. She couldn't let them down. Poor Ellen! She didn't stop to think that her parents would much rather see her honestly at the bottom, than dishonestly at the top!

Alicia was growing quite certain that it was Ellen who had taken the money. If not, why in the world was she always sneaking about by herself, listening outside doors, and doing such peculiar things? Neither of the purses had turned up. Nor had Belinda's money. Another purse and more missing money had not been traced either, and Emily had reported that her gold bar brooch, which her godmother had given her the term before, had also gone.

Emily was very tidy and careful and never lost things like Belinda or Irene. When Alicia heard her talking about her lost brooch in the common-room, she made up her mind to tell the others what she thought. Ellen, as usual, was not there. Out sneaking round somebody's door, I expect! thought Alicia.

'I say,' she said, raising her voice a little. 'Sally! I've got something to say about all these mysterious disappearances. I don't exactly want to accuse anyone – but I've been watching somebody lately, and they've been doing rather peculiar things.'

Everyone looked up in surprise. Sally looked round the common-room. 'Are we all here?' she said. 'Yes – wait though – Ellen isn't. We'll get her.'

'No, don't,' said Alicia. 'It would be as well not to.'

'What do you mean?' said Sally, puzzled. Then her eyes widened. 'Oh – you don't mean – no, Alicia, you don't mean that it's Ellen you've been watching! What has she been doing that's so peculiar?'

Alicia told how she had watched Ellen and seen her sneaking about in the passages, apparently waiting for a room to be empty. She related how she had found her going through Miss Parker's desk. Everyone listened, amazed.

'I wouldn't have thought it of her!' said Daphne, in a disgusted voice. 'What a thing to do! I never did like her. There's no doubt she took my purse and Gwen's – and Emily's brooch, and goodness knows how many things besides.'

'You're not to say that till we've proved something,' said Sally, sharply. 'We've no definite proof yet – and only Alicia, apparently, has seen Ellen sneaking about.'

'Well,' said Darrell, reluctantly, 'Sally, I noticed something once too. I found Ellen in Miss Potts' room, going through some things on her desk.'

'How dreadful!' said Daphne, and Gwen echoed her. Jean said nothing. She had been more friendly with Ellen than anyone else, though she had never been able to like her very much – but it seemed to her that Ellen was not quite the type of girl to become a thief. A thief! How terrible it sounded. Jean frowned. Surely Ellen couldn't be that!

'I don't think I believe it,' she said, slowly, in her clear Scots voice. 'She's a strange girl – but I don't think she's strange in that way.'

'Well, I bet she never gave you her games subscription!' said Alicia, remembering how Ellen had refused to go and get it.

'She did, the next time I asked her,' said Jean.

'Yes – and I bet it was after one of the purses had disappeared!' exclaimed Betty. Jean was silent. Yes, that was true. Ellen had not given up her subscription until the purses had gone. Things looked very black for Ellen.

'What are we to do?' said Darrell, helplessly. 'Sally, you're head-girl. What are you going to do?'

'I'll have to think about it,' said Sally. 'I can't decide this very minute.'

'There's nothing to decide!' said Alicia, with scorn in her voice. 'She's the thief. Well, tackle her with it and make her confess! If you don't, I shall!'

'No, you mustn't,' said Sally at once. 'I tell you, we've none of us got real proof – and it's a bad, wicked thing to do to accuse somebody without definite proof. You are not to say a word, Alicia. As head-girl I forbid you.'

Alicia's eyes sparkled wickedly. 'We'll see!' she said, and at that very moment who should come into the room but Ellen! She sensed hostility as soon as she came in and looked round, half scared.

The girls stared at her silently, rather taken-aback at her sudden appearance. Then Sally began to talk to Darrell and Jean turned to Emily. But Alicia was not going to change the subject, or to obey Sally either!

'Ellen,' she said, in a loud clear voice, 'What do you find when you go sneaking about in empty rooms and looking through desks?'

Ellen went pale. She stood perfectly still, her eyes glued on Alicia. 'What – what do you mean?' she stammered at last. Surely, surely nobody had guessed that she was looking for the exam papers!

'Shut up, Alicia!' said Sally, peremptorily. 'You know what I said.'

Alicia took no notice. 'You know jolly well what I mean, don't you?' she said to Ellen, in a hard voice. 'You know what you take when you creep into an empty room or go through somebody's desk or locker or drawer! Don't you?'

'I've never taken anything!' cried Ellen, a hunted look on her face. 'What should I take?'

'Oh – perhaps purses with money in – or a gold brooch or two,' drawled Alicia. 'Come on – own up, Ellen. You look as guilty as can be, so why deny it?'

Ellen stared as if she could not believe her eyes. She looked round at the quiet girls. Some of them could not

112

look at her. Mary-Lou was crying, for she hated scenes of this kind. Sally looked angrily and hopelessly at Alicia. It was no good stopping things now. They had gone too far. How dared Alicia defy her like that!

Darrell was angry, too, but her anger was partly directed at Ellen, whom she too thought looked exceedingly guilty. She was angry that Alicia had defied Sally, the head-girl – but after all – if Ellen was guilty, it was surely better that it should all be cleared up immediately?

'Do you mean that – that you think I've been stealing your things?' asked Ellen at last, with a great effort. 'You can't mean that!'

'We do,' said Alicia, grimly. 'Why else should you snoop round as you do? And why go through Miss Parker's desk? Can you give us a good explanation of that?'

No. Ellen couldn't. How could she say that she was hunting for the exam papers because she wanted to cheat. Oh, if once you started doing something wrong there was no end to it! She put her hands up to her face.

'I can't tell you anything,' she said, and tears made her fingers wet. 'But I didn't take your things. I didn't.'

'You *did*,' said Alicia. 'You're a coward as well as a thief. You can't even own up and give the things back!'

Ellen stumbled out of the room. The door shut behind her. Mary-Lou gave an unhappy sob. 'I'm so sorry for her!' she said. 'I can't help it! I am!'

16 In the middle of the night

There was a silence, only broken by Mary-Lou's sniffs. Most of the girls were upset and horrified. Alicia looked rather pleased with herself. Sally was tight-lipped and angry. Alicia looked at her and smiled maliciously.

'Sorry if I've upset you, Sally,' she said, 'but it was time we had it out with Ellen. As head-girl you should have done it yourself. As it was, you left it to me!'

'I did not!' said Sally. 'I forbade you to say anything. We shouldn't have accused Ellen – I know it's not right till we've got proof. And I wanted to think of the best way of doing it – not in front of everyone, that's certain!'

Darrell felt uncomfortably that Sally was right. It would have been best to wait a little, and think about it and then perhaps for Sally to have spoken with Ellen alone. Now the fat was in the fire! Everyone knew. Whatever would Ellen do!

'Well, all I can say is I'm grateful to Alicia for bringing the matter to a head,' said Daphne, shaking back her shining curls from her forehead. 'Perhaps our belongings will be safe now.'

'You ought to be loyal to Sally, not to Alicia,' flared up Darrell.

'Don't let's argue any more,' said Sally. 'The thing's done now, more's the pity. There's the supper-bell. For goodness' sake, let's go.'

They went soberly down to the supper-table. Ellen was not there. Jean asked about her.

'Shall I go and fetch Ellen, Miss Parker?' she said.

'No. She's got one of her headaches and has gone early to bed,' said Miss Parker. The girls exchanged looks. So Ellen couldn't even face them again that evening.

'Guilty conscience,' said Alicia to Betty, in a voice loud enough to reach Darrell and Sally.

Ellen was in bed when the form went up at their bed-time. She lay on her side, her face in the pillow, perfectly still. 'Pretending to be asleep,' said Alicia.

'Shut up,' said Jean, unexpectedly, in a low voice. 'You've done your bit already, Alicia Johns! We'll have no more jeering tonight. Hold your tongue.'

Alicia was taken-aback and glared at Jean. Jean glared back. Alicia said no more. Soon the girls were in bed and the lights were put out. They stopped talking at once. Sally had insisted that the rules were to be kept, and the girls respected her and kept them.

One by one they fell asleep. Daphne was one of the last to sleep, but long after she was asleep too, somebody else was wide awake. That was Ellen, of course.

She had gone to bed early for three reasons. One was that she really had got 'one of her headaches'. Another was that she didn't want to face the girls after their accusing faces. And the third was that she wanted to think.

She had hardly been able to believe her ears when the girls had accused her so unjustly. Ellen had not taken anything. She was completely honest in that way, however much she might have made up her mind to cheat over the exam. A thief! Alicia had called her that in front of everyone. It wasn't fair. It was most cruel and unjust!

But was it altogether unjust? After all, the girls, two of them at least, had seen her snooping round and had seen her going through Miss Parker's desk and looking through things on Miss Potts' desk too. It must seem to them as if such behaviour meant dishonesty – and it did mean dishonesty, though not the kind they accused her of.

What am I doing! How can I cheat like this! How can I be such a sneak and do such dreadful things! Ellen suddenly cried in her mind. What would Mother think of me! But oh, Mother, it's all because of you and Daddy that I want to do well. Not for myself. Surely it isn't so wrong if I cheat to please my parents, and not to please myself?

It *is* wrong, said her conscience. You know it is! See what your foolishness has led you into! You have been accused of something terrible – all because you were trying to do something wrong, and hadn't even done it!

I shan't cheat. I won't think of it any more, Ellen decided suddenly. I'll do badly in the papers and explain why to Mother. I will, I will!

Then the girls came up and she heard Alicia's spiteful remark. 'Pretending to be asleep.' In a flash she remembered her unkind accusations, her sneering words, and she remembered too how all the girls seemed to be against her and to believe she was wicked and bad.

Anger crept through her. How dared they accuse her wrongly, without any real proof at all? They all thought her bad, and nothing would convince them that she wasn't, she was sure. Very well, then, she *would* be bad! She

116

would cheat! She'd get up in the middle of the night and go and find those papers. She knew where they were – in Mam'zelle's room.

Ellen lay there in the darkness, her mind going over everything again and again. She felt defiant and obstinate now. She was labelled 'bad' by the girls. Then she *would* be bad. She'd enjoy it now! She would read those exam papers, and then she would look up all the answers, and she would surprise everyone by coming out top with practically perfect marks! That would make them all sit up!

She had no difficulty at all in lying awake until she was sure that the staff had gone to bed. Her eyes looked straight up into the darkness, and her head felt hot. She clenched her fists when she thought of Alicia's scornful face.

At last she thought it would be safe to get up. She sat up in bed and looked round. The moon was up and a ray pierced the darkness of the room. There was no movement anywhere, and all she could hear was the regular breathing of the other girls. She slid out of bed. She put her feet into her bedroom slippers and pulled her dressing-gown round her. Her heart was beating painfully.

She crept out of the room. She knocked against one of the beds on the way and held her breath in case she awoke the girl asleep there. But there was no movement.

She made her way down the moonlit passage, and down the stairs to Mam'zelle's room, the one she shared with Miss Potts. It was in darkness. Mam'zelle had gone to bed long ago.

Ellen went to the window to make sure that the

curtains were tightly drawn. She did not want anyone to see even a crack of light there at that time of night. They were thick curtains and shut out the moonlight. Then she shut the door and switched on the electric light.

She went to the desk. It was untidy as usual, for Mam'zelle Dupont, unlike Mam'zelle Rougier, could never keep her books and papers in neat order. Ellen began to go through the papers on top of the desk.

She went through them twice. The exam papers were not there! Her heart stood still. Surely they must be there. Perhaps they were *in* the desk. She hoped it was not locked. She had seen Mam'zelle lock it sometimes.

She tried it. Yes – it *was* locked. What a blow! Mam'zelle must have locked the test-papers up! Ellen sat down, her knees shaking with the suspense. Then her eyes caught sight of a key lying in the pen-tray. She snatched it up. She fitted it into the desk – and it opened! How like Mam'zelle to lock the desk carefully and leave the key in the pen-tray!

With trembling hands Ellen looked through the vast collection of papers there. In a corner, neatly banded together by Miss Parker, were the second-form test-papers!

With a thankful sigh Ellen took them up. She was just about to look carefully through them when she heard a sound. Her heart almost stopped! In a moment she slipped to the door and switched off the light. Then she shut the desk quietly and went over to the door to listen.

The sound came again. What was it? Was it somebody walking about? She would have to be very careful if so. She stuffed the papers into the big pocket of her dressing-gown and held them there. She had better get out of Mam'zelle's room if she could, because if anyone found her there she would get into very serious trouble.

Upstairs, in the dormy, just after Ellen had crept out, Darrell awoke. It was her bed that Ellen had bumped into, and she had not awakened immediately. But she sat up half a minute after Ellen had gone out of the room, wondering what had awakened her.

She was just about to settle down again when she noticed Ellen's empty bed. The moon was sending a bright ray down on it – and there was no lump there to show that Ellen was lying asleep. It was flat and empty!

Darrell stared at the empty bed. Where was Ellen? Was she ill again? Or – was she doing a bit more snooping to see if she could find anything valuable?

Darrell looked across at Sally. She ought to tell Sally and let her deal with it. Alicia had already interfered enough, and she, Darrell, ought to let Sally say what was to be done about the empty bed, if Ellen didn't come back very quickly.

Ellen didn't come back. Darrell waited impatiently for some minutes and then decided to try to find her. She wouldn't wake Sally. She was full of curiosity and wanted to follow Ellen herself. It seemed an exciting thing to do in the middle of the night!

She put on her slippers and dressing-gown. She went out of the room, treading quietly in her soft slippers. She stood in the passage and listened. She could hear nothing.

She padded down the passage and came to the stairs. Perhaps Ellen was going through the desks in the second-form room – or even in the first form! She went quietly down the stairs. She came to the first-form room, which had its door shut. Darrell opened it. The room was in darkness and she shut the door again. It made a little click.

She went to the second-form room and opened the door there. She thought she heard something and switched on the light quickly. She could see no one there. She switched off the light again and was about to shut the door when she thought she heard a sound. She quickly switched the light on again – and then, over by the cupboard she saw a movement! Just as if someone had pulled the door to very quickly.

Darrell's heart beat. Was it Ellen in there? Or somebody else? She wouldn't like it at all if it was a burglar. But it must be Ellen. She had gone from her bed and was nowhere to be seen. She must be there, in the cupboard, hiding.

Darrell went swiftly to the cupboard and gave the door a sharp tug. It came open – and there, crouching in the cupboard, scared and trembling, was Ellen! She had slipped out of Mam'zelle's room and gone into the second-form room when she had heard Darrell coming. She had hidden in the cupboard, as still as a mouse.

Darrell looked in amazement at her. 'Come out!' she said. 'You bad girl, Ellen! Have you been stealing something again?'

'No,' said Ellen, and came out. She held on to the test-papers in her pocket, and Darrell noticed the action.

'What have you got there?' she demanded. 'Show me! Quick! You're hiding something.'

'I'm not! I'm not!' cried Ellen, forgetting all about

being quiet. Darrell tried to snatch Ellen's hand away from her pocket, and Ellen, afraid, lashed out at Darrell with her other hand. It caught her on the face.

Then Darrell lost her temper! She flew at Ellen, shook her fiercely, and screamed at her! Ellen fell over the legs of a desk and dragged Darrell down with her. She struggled and Darrell scolded her well. 'You wicked girl! Coming out and stealing things! You give me what you've taken!'

Ellen suddenly went limp. She could not struggle any longer. Darrell was able to drag her up and make her take her hand away from her pocket. She pulled out the packet of papers roughly. The band broke and they scattered all over the floor. Ellen covered her face and began to sob loudly.

Darrell stared at the papers and picked one or two up. 'So you cheat too, do you?' she said, in a scornful voice. 'Tomorrow's exam papers! Ellen Wilson, what sort of a girl are you? A thief and a cheat! How dare you come here to Malory Towers?'

'Oh, put the papers back and don't let anyone know!' sobbed Ellen. 'Oh, don't tell anyone!'

'I'll certainly put the papers back,' said Darrell, grimly. 'But as for not telling anyone, that's absurd!'

She dragged Ellen to the door. 'Where did you find the papers? In Mam'zelle's desk. We'll put them back there then.'

She put them back, and then, with trembling fingers, Ellen locked the desk again. They went up to the dormy. All the girls were still asleep.

'Tomorrow,' said Darrell, 'I shall tell Sally, Ellen. And

she will decide what is to be done about you. I expect you'll be expelled. Now get into bed and try to go to sleep!'

17 Rumours and tales

Nobody heard the two girls coming back. No one guessed that Darrell and Ellen had been out of their beds and back again. Darrell, furious and excited, lay awake for some time, debating whether or not to wake Sally there and then and tell her what had happened.

'No, I won't,' she decided, reluctantly. 'It would only wake all the others, and I must get Sally alone and tell her.'

She suddenly fell asleep, and, tired out with excitement, slept very soundly indeed. But Ellen could not sleep at all. This was nothing new for her. Most nights she did not sleep until the early hours of the morning. Now she lay on her back in bed, quite stunned by all the night's happenings. But gradually she ceased to worry about them for a bigger trouble came upon her. Her headache grew so bad that she thought her head must surely burst! Red hot hammers seemed at work inside it and at last the girl grew really frightened.

What was happening to her? Was she going mad? Was this what it felt like? She lay perfectly still with her eyes closed, hoping that the pain would die down. But it didn't. It got worse.

At last it was so bad that she began to moan softly. The thought of kind, comforting Matron came to her. Matron! Matron had been kind to her in the san. She would be kind now. Ellen felt that if she could only have one small bit of kindness from someone she would feel better.

She sat up painfully, her head spinning round. The moon was now shining fully into the dormy. She could see all the white beds with their quilts slipping off, or neatly pulled up. The girls lay in various positions, fast asleep.

Ellen got out of bed slowly, because any quick movement made her head hurt unbearably. She forgot about her dressing-gown, she forgot about her slippers. She made her way slowly to the door as if she was walking in her sleep. She passed out of it like a little ghost in pyjamas.

How she found her way to Matron's room she never remembered. But Matron suddenly awoke from sleep to hear a soft knocking at her door that went on and on.

'Come in!' she cried, 'Who is it?' She switched on the light. But nobody came in. The soft knocking went on and on. Matron was puzzled and a little alarmed.

'Come in!' she called again. But nobody came. Matron leaped out of bed and went to the door, a sturdy figure in a voluminous night-dress. She flung the door open – and there stood poor Ellen, drooping like a weeping willow tree, her hand up as if she was still knocking at the door.

'Ellen! What's the matter, child? Are you ill?' cried

Matron and pulled her gently into her room.

'My head,' said Ellen, in a tired whisper. 'It's bursting, Matron.'

It didn't take Matron long to deal with Ellen. Seeing that the girl was in great pain, and that she could hardly even open her eyes, Matron soon had her in a warm and comfortable bed in a little room opening off her own. She gave her medicine and a hot drink. She put a comforting hot-water bottle in beside her. She was kind and gentle and spoke in a very low voice so as not to jar Ellen's aching head.

'Now you go to sleep,' she said. 'You'll feel better in the morning.'

Ellen did fall asleep. Matron stood by the bed and looked down at her. She was puzzled. There was something wrong with this girl. She was worrying secretly about something, as she had been doing before, when she was in the san. Perhaps it would be better for her to go home for a while.

In the morning Darrell woke up with the others when the dressing-bell went. She sat up, remembering all the excitement of the night. She glanced at Sally. She must somehow get her alone.

Then Sally gave an exclamation. 'Where's Ellen? Her bed's empty!'

Everyone looked at Ellen's empty bed. 'Perhaps she got up early,' suggested Emily. 'We'll see her at breakfast-time.'

Darrell felt a bit worried. Had Ellen got up early? Where was she?

Ellen was not at breakfast, of course. The girls looked

125

at the empty place, and Darrell felt distinctly uncomfortable. Surely – surely Ellen hadn't run away in the night and not come back! Mam'zelle was taking breakfast that day and Darrell spoke to her.

'Where's Ellen, Mam'zelle?'

'She is not coming to breakfast,' said Mam'zelle, who knew nothing more than that. Miss Parker had told her hurriedly as she passed her in the corridor. 'I do not know why. Perhaps she is ill.'

Now Alicia began to feel uncomfortable too. She remembered how she had accused Ellen so bitterly the day before. Where *was* Ellen? She too began to wonder if the girl had run away home. She ate her porridge rather silently.

The next piece of news came from a first-former, Katie. She had heard Miss Parker talking to Miss Potts, and had caught a few words.

'I say! What's up with Ellen Wilson?' she demanded. 'I heard Nosey tell Potty that she was going to be sent home! What's she done?'

Sent home! The second-formers looked at one another. Did that mean that the staff had found out about Ellen – had perhaps discovered she had been stealing? And she was to be expelled! Good gracious!

'She's either been found out by one of the mistresses, or else she's gone and confessed,' said Alicia, at last. 'We'd better not say too much about what we know. It's not much to the credit of the school. I expect it will be all hushed up.'

'Do you mean that you really think Ellen is being sent away – expelled from the school – because she stole those things?' said Daphne, looking suddenly white. 'Surely she won't!'

'She jolly well will,' said Betty, and there was such scorn in her voice that Daphne looked quite startled. 'And a good thing too! Fancy having that kind of girl at Malory Towers!'

Darrell was bewildered by the turn things had taken. Now she didn't know whether to report the happenings of last night or not. If Ellen was to be sent home for stealing, then there didn't seem much point in telling anyone that she, Darrell, had caught her cheating – taking the test-papers to look at before the test. Because certainly Ellen wouldn't take the tests now, and why blacken her name even more, now that she was apparently being sent off in disgrace?

Darrell was a generous girl, even to those she considered her enemies. She thought over the night before. She had certainly given Ellen a good deal of punishment for cheating! She felt rather hot when she remembered how she had shaken Ellen and screamed at her. That was her temper again, of course. Sally wouldn't have done a thing like that. Sally would have dealt with the whole thing in a dignified, calm way, and would have made Ellen show her the test-papers without a lot of undignified rough behaviour that ended in both girls rolling on the floor!

I don't manage things very well, somehow, thought Darrell, rubbing her nose with her hand. I just go off the deep end with a splash! I fly off the handle, I go up in smoke! Well, what am I going to do? Tell Sally or not?

She decided not to. There didn't seem any point at all

in complaining about Ellen, and making her character still worse if she was really going to be sent home. So Darrell held her tongue, a thing that not many of the second form would have done in the circumstances, for most of them dearly loved a gossip.

Still, there was plenty of gossip in the second form about Ellen. Everyone seemed to take it for granted that somehow or other it had been found out by the staff that Ellen had taken the purses, money and brooch and possibly other things as well, and was being expelled for that.

Curiously enough, one of the girls who seemed most distressed about this was Daphne. 'But surely they won't expel her without some proof?' she kept saying. 'Sally, Darrell, you said to Alicia yesterday that there was no real proof that Ellen had stolen anything. What will happen to Ellen? Will another school take her?'

'I don't know. I shouldn't think so,' said Alicia. 'She's finished! Serve her right!'

'Don't be so hard,' said Jean. 'Don't think I'm standing up for her – I'm not. But you always sound so hard and unmerciful, Alicia.'

'Well, I was right yesterday when I accused Ellen, wasn't I?' demanded Alicia. 'You were all so soft you didn't want to have it out with her! Good thing I did.'

The second form decided to say nothing about Ellen to the staff. If Miss Grayling was going to expel the girl, she would want to keep it quiet. So the less said the better.

So, rather to Miss Parker's surprise, nobody asked about Ellen at all. Curious, this lack of interest, she thought, and she said nothing either. The girls had no idea at all when or if Ellen had gone home, though somebody passed round a rumour that a car had been seen in the drive that morning. Perhaps it had come to fetch Ellen!

It hadn't. It was the doctor's car. He had been called in to examine the girl, and he had spoken gravely to Matron and Miss Grayling. 'There's something here I don't understand. Is the child worried about anything? Is there anything wrong at her home? Has anything upset her at school?'

Neither Matron nor the Head Mistress could give the doctor any information. As far as they knew there was nothing wrong at Ellen's home, and there had been no upset in her form. Miss Parker was called in and she too said that as far as she knew Ellen had not been in any trouble in any class, except for mild tickings-off for not doing work up to standard.

'We think, Ellen,' said Miss Grayling gently, when the doctor had gone, 'we think you should go home when you feel well enough. That would be the best place for you now.'

She was startled by Ellen's response to this suggestion. The girl sat up and pushed back her hair in a despairing way. 'Oh, no, Miss Grayling! Don't expel me! Please don't!'

'Expel you!' said the Head, in amazement. 'What do you mean?'

Ellen had broken into sobs and Matron came hurrying up at once, making signs to Miss Grayling to go. 'She mustn't be excited in any way,' she whispered. 'So sorry,

129

Miss Grayling, but I think you'd better go. I'll deal with her now.'

Miss Grayling, very puzzled indeed, went quietly out of the room. Why should Ellen think she was going to be expelled? There was something here that needed looking into.

It took Ellen a long time to calm down. She really thought that Miss Grayling's suggestion of going home meant that she was telling her she was to be sent away from Malory Towers – expelled in disgrace. Perhaps Darrell had been to her and told her about the cheating? Or perhaps Alicia had told her that they all believed she had been stealing, and Miss Grayling had decided to expel her because of that. Ellen didn't know. She began to worry all over again and Matron was alarmed at the quick rise in her temperature.

Some of the second-formers were upset at the thought that Ellen might have been already expelled, and had been sent home without even saying good-bye. Mary-Lou especially was upset. She hadn't liked Ellen very much, but she was very sorry for her. She spoke to Daphne about it at break.

'Daphne, isn't it awful? What will poor Ellen say to her parents when she gets home? Do you think she will have to tell them herself that she's been sent away for stealing?'

'Don't!' said Daphne. 'Don't let's talk about it, Mary-Lou. Look, we've got about ten minutes, haven't we? I've got a most important parcel to send off this morning, and I can't find any string anywhere. Be a dear and get me some. I've got the brown paper.'

Mary-Lou sped off, wondering what the important parcel was. She couldn't seem to find any string at all. It was astonishing, the total lack of any string that morning! When at last she got back to Daphne, the bell went for the next lesson.

'Haven't you got any string?' said Daphne, disappointed. 'Oh, blow! Well, I'll see if I can find some after the morning lessons, and then I'll slip down to the post with the parcel this afternoon. I've got half an hour in between two lessons, because my music-mistress isn't here today.'

'Is it so very important?' asked Mary-Lou. 'I could run with it for you, if you like.'

'No. You'd never get there and back in time,' said Daphne. 'It's a long way by the inland road. You could manage it by the coast road, but there's such a gale again today you'd be blown over the top! I'll go in between lessons this afternoon.'

But she couldn't go after all, with her 'important parcel', whatever it was, for the music-mistress turned up, and Daphne was called away to her lesson. She left the parcel in her desk.

'Oh dear!' she said at tea-time, to Gwen and Mary-Lou. 'I did so badly want to take my parcel to the post – and I had to have my music-lesson after all – and now I've got to go to Miss Parker after tea for a returned lesson, and after that there's a rehearsal for that silly French play.'

'What's so urgent about the parcel?' asked Gwen. 'Somebody's birthday?'

Daphne hesitated. 'Yes,' she said. 'That's it. If it

doesn't go today it won't get there in time!'

'Well, you'll have to post it tomorrow,' said Gwen. Mary-Lou looked at Daphne's worried face. What a pity she, Mary-Lou, couldn't take it for her. She always liked doing things for Daphne, and getting that charming smile in return.

She began to think how she might do it. I'm free at seven, after prep, she thought. I'll have half an hour before supper. I could never get to the post-office and back if I take the inland road – but I could if I took the coast road. Would I dare to – in the dark and rain?

She thought about it as she sat in afternoon school. People don't mind what they do for their friends, she thought. They dare anything. Daphne would be so thrilled if I went to the post and got her birthday parcel off for her. How kind she is to want it to get there on the day. Just like her. Well – if it isn't too dark and horrible, I might run along tonight for her. I mustn't tell anyone though, because it's against the rules. If Sally got to know, she'd forbid me!

So timid little Mary-Lou planned to do something that even not one of the seniors would do on a dark, windy night – take the coast road on the cliff, whilst a gale blew wildly round!

18 Mary-Lou

After prep that night Mary-Lou scuttled back to the second-form room, which was now empty except for Gwendoline, who was tidying up.

Mary-Lou went to Daphne's desk. Gwendoline looked at her jealously. 'What do you want in Daphne's desk? I can take her anything she's forgotten. I wish you wouldn't suck up to her so much, Mary-Lou.'

'I don't,' said Mary-Lou. She opened the desk-lid and fished for the brown-paper parcel, now neatly tied up with string. 'I'm going to the post with this for Daphne! But don't go and split on me, Gwen. I know it's against the rules.'

Gwendoline stared at Mary-Lou in surprise. '*You* breaking the rules!' she said. 'I don't believe you ever did that before. You're mad to think you can get to the post and back in time.'

'I shall. I'm taking the coast road,' said Mary-Lou, valiantly, though her heart failed her when she said it. 'It's only ten minutes there and back by that road.'

'Mary-Lou! You must be daft!' said Gwendoline. 'There's a gale blowing and it's dark as pitch. You'll be blown over the cliff as sure as anything.'

'I shan't,' said Mary-Lou, stoutly, though again her heart sank inside her. 'And, anyway, it's only a small thing to do for a friend. I know Daphne particularly wants this parcel to go today.'

'Daphne isn't your friend,' said Gwendoline, a flare

of jealously coming up in her again.

'She is,' said Mary-Lou, with such certainly that Gwendoline was annoyed.

'Baby!' said Gwendoline, scornfully. 'You're too silly even to see that Daphne only uses you because you can help her with her French. That's the only reason she puts up with you hanging round her. She's told me so.'

Mary-Lou stood looking at Gwendoline, the parcel in her hand. She felt suddenly very miserable. 'It's not true,' she said. 'You're making it up.'

'It *is* true!' said Gwendoline, spitefully. 'I tell you Daphne has said so herself to me heaps of times. What would a girl like Daphne want with a mouse like you! You're just useful to her, that's all, and if you weren't so jolly conceited you'd know it without being told!'

Mary-Lou felt as if it must be true. Gwendoline would never say such a thing so emphatically if it wasn't. She picked up the parcel, her mouth quivering, and turned to go.

'Mary-Lou! You don't mean to say you're going to bother with that parcel after what I've just told you!' called Gwendoline, in surprise. 'Don't be an idiot.'

'I'm taking it for Daphne because I'm *her* friend!' answered Mary-Lou, in a shaky voice. 'She may not be mine, but if I'm hers I'll still be willing to do things for her.'

'Stupid little donkey!' said Gwendoline to herself, and began to slam books back on to shelves and to make a terrific cloud of dust with the blackboard duster.

She didn't tell Daphne that Mary-Lou had gone off into the darkness with her parcel. She was feeling rather ashamed of having been so outspoken. Daphne might not like it. But after all it was nearly the end of the term, and there would be now no need for Mary-Lou to help Daphne. She would probably be glad to be rid of Mary-Lou when she no longer needed her help with her French.

Half-past seven came and the supper-bell rang. Girls poured out of the different rooms and went clattering down to the dining-room. 'Oooh! Coffee tonight for a change! And jammy buns and rolls and potted meat!'

They all sat down and helped themselves, whilst Miss Parker poured out big cups of coffee. She glanced round the table. 'Two empty chairs! Who's missing? Oh, Ellen, of course. Who's the other?'

'Mary-Lou,' said Sally. 'I saw her just after prep. She'll be along in a minute, Miss Parker.'

But five minutes, ten minutes went by and there was no sign of Mary-Lou. Miss Parker frowned.

'Surely she must have heard the bell. See if you can find her, Sally.'

Sally sped off and came back to report that Mary-Lou was nowhere to be found. By this time Gwendoline was in a great dilemma. She and she only knew where Mary-Lou was. If she told, she would get Mary-Lou into trouble. Surely she would be back soon? Maybe she had had to wait at the post-office!

Then she suddenly remembered something. The post-office shut at seven! It wouldn't be any use Mary-Lou trying to post a parcel there, because it would be shut. Why hadn't she thought of that before? Then what had happened to Mary-Lou?

A cold hand seemed to creep round Gwendoline's heart

and almost stop her breathing. Suppose – suppose that the wind had blown little Mary-Lou over the cliff? Suppose that even now she was lying on the rocks, dead or badly hurt! The thought was so terrible that Gwendoline couldn't swallow her morsel of bun and half choked.

Daphne thumped her on the back. Gwendoline spoke to her in a low, urgent voice.

'Daphne! I must tell you something as soon after supper as possible. Come into one of the practice-rooms where we shall be alone.'

Daphne looked alarmed. She nodded. When supper was finished she led the way to one of the deserted practice-rooms and switched on the light. 'What's the matter?' she asked Gwendoline. 'You look like a ghost.'

'It's Mary-Lou. I know where she went,' said Gwendoline.

'Well, why on earth didn't you tell Miss Parker then?' asked Daphne, crossly. 'What *is* the matter, Gwen?'

'Daphne, she took your precious parcel to the post just after seven o'clock,' said Gwendoline. 'She took the coast road. Do you think anything's happened to her?'

Daphne took this in slowly. 'Took my parcel to the post? What*ever* for! At this time of night, too.'

'She went all soppy and said that although it meant her going out in the dark and the wind, she'd do it because you were her friend,' said Gwendoline.

'Why didn't you stop her, you idiot?' demanded Daphne.

'I did try,' said Gwendoline. 'I even told her that you were *not* her friend – you only found her useful for helping you with your French, as you've often and often told me, Daphne – and you'd think that would stop anyone from going off into the dark on a windy night, wouldn't you, to post a silly parcel?'

'And didn't it stop her?' said Daphne, in a strange sort of voice.

'No. She just said that she would take it for you because she was *your* friend,' said Gwendoline, rather scornfully. 'She said you might not be her friend, but she was yours, and she'd still be willing to do things for you.'

Gwendoline was amazed to see tears suddenly glisten in Daphne's eyes. Daphne never cried! 'What's up?' said Gwendoline in surprise.

'Nothing that you'd understand,' said Daphne, blinking the tears away savagely. 'Good heavens! Fancy going out on a night like this and taking the coast road – just because she wanted to take that parcel for me. And the post-office would be shut too! Poor little Mary-Lou! What can have happened to her?'

'Has she fallen over the cliff, do you think?' asked Gwendoline.

Daphne went very white. 'No – no, don't say that!' she said. 'You can't think how awful that would be. I'd never, never forgive myself!'

'It wouldn't be *your* fault if she did,' said Gwendoline, surprised at this outburst.

'It would, it would! You don't understand!' cried Daphne. 'Oh, poor kind little Mary-Lou! And you sent her out thinking I didn't like her – that I only just used her! I *do* like her. I like her ten times better than I like you! She's kind and generous and unselfish. I know I did use her at first, and welcomed her just because she could help me – but I couldn't help getting fond of her. She just gives everything and asks nothing!'

'But – you told me heaps of times you only put up with her because she was useful,' stammered Gwendoline, completely taken aback by all this, and looking very crestfallen indeed.

'I know I did! I was beastly. It was the easiest thing to do, to keep you from bothering me and nagging me about Mary-Lou. Oh, I shall never, never get over it if anything has happened! I'm going after her. I'm going to see if I can find her!'

'You can't!' cried Gwendoline, in horror. 'Hark at the wind! It's worse than ever!'

'If Mary-Lou can go out into that wind to post a stupid parcel for me, surely *I* can go out into it to find her!' said Daphne, and a look came into her pretty, pale face that Gwendoline had never seen before – a sturdy, determined look that gave her face unexpected character.

'But, Daphne,' protested Gwendoline, feebly, and then stopped. Daphne had gone out of the little music-room like a whirlwind. She ran up to the dormy and got her mackintosh. She tore down to the cloak-room and put on her Wellingtons. Nobody saw her. Then out she went into the night, flashing on her torch to see her way.

It was a wild night, and the wind howled round fiercely. It took Daphne's breath away as she made her way to the coast road up on the cliff. Whatever would it be like there! She would be almost blown away.

She flashed her torch here and there. There was nothing to be seen but a few bent bushes, dripping with rain.

She went a little farther and began to call loudly and desperately.

'Mary-Lou! Mary-LOU! Where are you?'

The wind tore her words out of her mouth and flung them over the cliff. She called again, putting her hands up to her mouth. 'Mary-Lou! MARY-LOU! MARY-LOU!'

And surely that was a faint call in answer. 'Here! Here! Help me!'

19 A heroine!

Daphne stood quite still and listened. The cry came again on the wind, very faint. 'Here! Here!'

It seemed to come from somewhere in front. Daphne struggled on against the wind, and then came to a place where the cliff edge swung inwards. She followed the edge round cautiously, not daring to go too near, for the wind was so strong. Still, it seemed to be dying down a little now.

She suddenly heard Mary-Lou's voice much nearer. 'Help! Help!'

Daphne was afraid of being blown over the cliff if she went too near the edge. But the voice seemed to come from the edge somewhere. Daphne sat down on the wet ground, feeling that the wind would not then have so much power over her and began to edge herself forward, holding on the tufts of grass when she could.

She came to where the cliff had crumbled away a little, and made a series of ledges, going steeply down to the sea. She crawled to this place, lay flat down and shone her light over the broken cliff.

And there, a few feet below, was poor Mary-Lou, clinging for dear life to a ledge, her white face upturned to the glare of the torch.

'Help!' she called again, feebly, seeing the torch. 'Oh, help me! I can't hold on much longer!'

Daphne was horrified. She could see that if Mary-Lou did leave go, she would hurtle down to the rocks a long way below. Her heart went cold at the thought. What could she do?

'I'm here, Mary-Lou!' she called. 'Hold on. I'll fetch help.'

'Oh – Daphne! Is it you! Don't go away, Daphne. I shall fall in a minute. Can't you do something?'

Daphne looked down at Mary-Lou. She felt that it would not be the slightest use leaving her and going for help for it was clear that Mary-Lou might leave go at any moment. No, she must think of something else and do it at once.

She thought of her mackintosh belt, and her tunic belt. If she tied those both together and let them down, Mary-Lou might hold them and drag herself up. But would they reach?

She undid her mackintosh belt and took off her tunic belt with fingers that fumbled exasperatingly. All the time she kept up a comforting flow of words to Mary-Lou.

140

'I'll save you, don't you worry! I'll soon have you up here! I'm making a rope with my belts and I'll let it down. Hold on, Mary-Lou, hold on, and I'll soon save you!'

Mary-Lou was comforted and held on. She had been so frightened when the gale took her and rolled her over and over to the edge of the cliff. How she had managed to hold on to the tufts of grass she didn't know. It had seemed ages and ages till she heard Daphne's voice. Now Daphne was here and would rescue her. Whatever Gwendoline had said, Daphne was her friend!

Daphne lay down flat again. She found a stout gorse bush behind her and she pushed her legs under it till her feet found the sturdy root-stem growing out of the ground. Heedless of scratches and pricks, she wound her two feet firmly round the stem, so that she had a good hold with her legs and would not be likely to be pulled over the cliff by Mary-Lou.

A frantic voice suddenly came up to her. 'Daphne! This tuft of grass is giving way! I shall fall! Quick, quick.'

Daphne hurriedly let down the rough rope, made of her two belts. Mary-Lou caught at it and looped the end firmly round her wrists. Daphne felt the pull at once.

'Are you all right?' she called, anxiously. 'You won't fall now, will you?'

'No. I don't think so. My feet have got quite a firm hold,' called back Mary-Lou, much reassured by the belt round her wrists. 'I shan't pull you over, shall I, Daphne?

'No. But I don't think I'm strong enough to pull you up!' said Daphne, in despair. 'And the belts might break and let you fall. I don't see that we can do anything but just hang on to each other till somebody finds us.'

'Oh, poor Daphne! This is awful for you,' came back Mary-Lou's voice. 'I wish I'd never thought of taking that parcel.'

'It was kind of you,' said Daphne, not knowing how to get the words out. 'But you're always kind, Mary-Lou. And Mary-Lou, I'm your friend. You know that, don't you? Gwen told me the beastly things she said. They're not true. I think the world of you, I do really. I've never been fond of anyone before.'

'Oh, I knew Gwen told me untruths, as soon as I heard your voice and knew you'd come to look for me,' said Mary-Lou, out of the darkness. 'I think you're a heroine, Daphne.'

'I'm not,' said Daphne. 'I'm a beastly person. You simply don't know how beastly.'

'This is a funny conversation to be having on a cliff-side in a stormy night, isn't it?' said Mary-Lou, trying to sound cheerful. 'Oh dear – I am so sorry to have caused all this trouble. Daphne, when will people come to look for us?'

'Well, only Gwen knows I've come out,' said Daphne. 'If I don't come back soon, surely she will tell Nosey Parker, and they'll send out to look for us. I do hope she'll have the sense to tell someone.'

Gwendoline had. She had felt very worried indeed about first Mary-Lou and now Daphne. When Daphne had not come back after half an hour, Gwendoline had gone to Miss Parker. She told her where Mary-Lou had gone and that Daphne had gone to look for her.

'What! Out on the coast road at night! In this weather!

What madness!' cried Miss Parker, and rushed off to Miss Grayling at once.

In two or three minutes a search-party was out with lanterns, ropes and flasks of hot cocoa. It was not long before the two girls were found. Miss Grayling gave an agonized exclamation as she saw them. 'They might both have been killed!'

Daphne's arms were almost numb with strain when the search-party came up. They saw her lying flat on the ground, her legs curled tightly round the stem of the prickly bush, holding the two belts down the cliff-side – and there, at the other end, holding on for dear life, was Mary-Lou, the sea pounding away far below her.

A rope was let down to Mary-Lou, slipped right over her head, and tightened over arms and shoulders. Another one looped tightly round her waist. Daphne got up thankfully, her legs almost asleep, and Miss Parker caught hold of her. 'Steady now! Hold on to me!'

Mary-Lou was pulled up safely by a hefty gardener. She lay on the ground, crying with relief. The gardener undid the ropes and lifted her up. 'I'll carry her,' he said. 'Give her a drink. She's freezing!'

Both girls felt glad of the hot cocoa. Then, holding on to Miss Parker, Daphne staggered back to school, followed by the gardener carrying Mary-Lou, and then by the rest of the party.

'Put both girls to bed,' Miss Grayling said to Matron. 'They've had a terrible experience. I only hope they don't get pneumonia now! Daphne, you saved little Mary-Lou's life, there's no doubt about that. I am very proud of you!'

Daphne said nothing at all, but, to Miss Grayling's

surprise, hung her head and turned away. She had no time to puzzle over this, but helped Matron to get Mary-Lou undressed and into bed. Both girls were soon in warm beds, with hot food and drink inside them. They each felt extremely sleepy, and went off to sleep quite suddenly.

The second-formers were in bed, worried and sleepless. Gwen had told them about Mary-Lou going off, and Daphne following her to see if she could find her. They knew that a search-party had gone out. All kinds of horrible pictures came into their minds as they lay in bed and listened to the wind.

They talked long after lights out. Sally did not forbid them. This was not a usual night – it was a night of anxiety, and talking helped.

Then, after a long time, they heard Miss Parker's quick footsteps coming along the corridor. News! They all sat up at once.

She switched on the light and looked round at the seven waiting girls. Then she told them the story of how Mary-Lou and Daphne had been found, and how Daphne, by her ingenious idea, had saved Mary-Lou. She described how she had laid herself down on the wet ground, her feet curled round the gorse bush stem, and had held the belts down to Mary-Lou until help came.

'Daphne's a heroine!' cried Darrell. 'I never liked her – but, Miss Parker, she's been marvellous, hasn't she! She's a real heroine!'

'I think she is,' said Miss Parker. 'I did not guess that she had it in her. She's in bed now, in the san, but I think she'll soon be all right again. We'll give her three cheers and a clap when she comes back to class.'

She switched off the light and said goodnight. The girls talked excitedly for a few minutes more, thankful that they knew what had happened. Fancy Daphne turning out like that! And doing it for Mary-Lou! Why, Gwen had always said that Daphne only put up with Mary-Lou because she helped her with her French.

'Daphne must be fond of Mary-Lou,' said Darrell, voicing what everyone thought. 'I'm glad. I always thought it was mean to use Mary-Lou and not really like her.'

'I wonder what became of the parcel,' said Belinda 'Mary-Lou can't have posted it, because the post-office was shut. I bet nobody thought of the precious parcel.'

'We'll go and hunt for it tomorrow,' said Sally. 'I say – what a small dormy we are tonight – only seven of us. Ellen gone – and Daphne and Mary-Lou in the san. Well, thank goodness they're there and not out on the cliff.'

The wind rose to a gale again and howled round North Tower. The girls snuggled down closer into the beds. 'I do think Daphne was brave,' said Darrell, 'and I can't *imagine* how timid little Mary-Lou could possibly have dared to go out in this gale. *Mary-Lou* of all people.'

'People are strange,' said Irene. 'You simply never can tell what a person will do from one day to the next.'

'You never said a truer word!' chuckled Darrell. 'Today you put your French grammar away in the games cupboard and tried to put your lacrosse stick into your desk – and goodness knows what you'll do tomorrow.'

20 An astonishing parcel

It was difficult to do tests in the midst of so much excitement. The story of Mary-Lou and Daphne ran through the school and everyone talked about it. The two girls did not appear in school that day, because Matron was keeping them quiet. They neither of them seemed any the worse for their adventure.

Before afternoon school Darrell, Sally, Irene and Belinda set off up the cliff-path to look for the parcel. The wind had completely died down and it was a lovely day, one of Cornwall's best. The sky was as blue as a cornflower, and the sea picked up the colour and made the view a really beautiful one, as the girls walked up the coast-path.

'Look – that must be where Mary-Lou was blown over,' said Darrell, pointing to where the cliff had crumbled. 'And see – surely that's the gorse bush Daphne wound her legs round. Golly, she must have been scratched!'

The girls stood and looked at the place where Mary-Lou and Daphne had had their frightening adventure. Sally shivered, thinking of what it must have been like in the dark night, with the wind howling round and the sea pounding on the rocks below.

'It's horrid to think of,' she said. 'Come on – let's hunt about for the parcel. Mary-Lou must have dropped it somewhere near here, I should think.'

They began to look. It was Darrell who found the parcel, lying wet and torn in the grass some little way off.

'I've got it!' she shouted, and ran to pick it up. 'Oh, it's all coming to pieces. The paper is pulpy, and the contents are coming out!'

'Better take off the paper and carry the things inside home in our hands,' said Sally. So Darrell stripped off the wet, pulpy paper and shook out the contents. They fell on the grass.

They were rather odd. The girls looked at them, lying there. There were four purses of different sizes and shapes. There were three boxes, the kind that brooches or lockets are sold in by jewellers – little leather boxes with a catch you had to press to open them.

Darrell picked one up and pressed it. It shot open – and a little gold bar brooch gleamed inside. She looked at it, bewildered, then passed it to Sally.

'Isn't that Emily's brooch – the one she lost?'

'It's got her name behind it if it is,' said Sally, in a sober voice. She took out the brooch and looked at the back of the little gold bar.

'Yes – it's Emily's,' she said. 'Her name is there.'

Sally opened another of the boxes. It contained a little gold necklace, plain and simple.

'Katie's!' said Irene at once. 'I've seen her wearing it! Good gracious – how did these come to be in the parcel? Is it the right parcel we've found?'

Sally picked everything up from the grass. Her face looked very serious. 'It's the right parcel,' she said. 'Look – these purses belong to people we know. That's Gwen's. And that's Mary-Lou's. And that's surely Betty's.'

The four girls looked at one another in bewilderment. 'If this was the parcel that Mary-Lou was posting for Daphne, how was it Daphne put all these things into it?' said Sally, voicing what everyone was thinking.

'Could she have got them from Ellen?' said Darrell, puzzled. 'We all know Ellen must have taken them. Wherever did she get them from? Is she doing it to shield Ellen, or something?'

'We'll have to find out,' said Irene. 'Sally, we'd better take the parcel to Miss Grayling. We can't keep this to ourselves.'

'No, we can't,' said Sally. 'We'll go back at once.'

They went back, saying very little, puzzled and solemn. Here were the stolen things, the things they had accused Ellen of taking – Daphne had somehow got hold of them and for some extraordinary reason was sending them away – and Mary-Lou had almost lost her life in trying to post them, and had been rescued by Daphne! It was all most complicated.

'I think it's all very mysterious,' said Belinda. 'I can't make head or tail of it. It's a pity Ellen's been expelled, or we might go to her and show her what we've found.'

The girls had no idea that Ellen was still at Malory Towers. What with one rumour and another they were all firmly convinced she had been sent home!

The bell was ringing for afternoon school as they got in. They caught Miss Parker as she was going to the second form and asked her for permission to go and see Miss Grayling.

'We've found the parcel that Mary-Lou went to post

and we think we ought to hand it over to Miss Grayling,' explained Sally.

'Very well. Don't be too long,' said Miss Parker, and went on her way. The four girls went to Miss Grayling's part of the buildings and knocked at her door.

'Come in!' said her low voice, and they opened the door and went in. She was alone. She looked up in surprise when she saw four girls. Then she smiled, for she liked all of them, even harum-scarum Belinda.

'Please, Miss Grayling, we found the parcel that Mary-Lou went to post for Daphne,' said Sally, coming forward. 'And here are the things that were inside it. The paper was so wet that we had to take it off.'

She placed the purses and the boxes down on the Head Mistress's desk. Miss Grayling looked at them in surprise. 'Were *these* inside!' she said. 'Are they all Daphne's, then? I understand that it was Daphne's parcel.'

There was an awkward pause. 'Well, Miss Grayling, they are things belonging to us girls,' said Sally, at last. 'We missed them at various times. Some of the purses had money in when they were taken. They are empty now.'

Miss Grayling suddenly looked quite different. A stern expression came into her eyes, and she sat up straight.

'You will have to explain a little better, Sally,' she said. 'Am I to understand that these were stolen at some time from one or other of you this term?'

'Yes, Miss Grayling,' said Sally, and the others nodded.

'You think Daphne took them?' said Miss Grayling, after a pause. The girls looked at one another.

'Well,' said Sally at last, 'we did think Ellen had taken

them, Miss Grayling. We knew she had been expelled, you see – and we thought . . .'

'Wait!' said Miss Grayling, in such a sharp tone that the four girls jumped. 'Ellen *expelled*! Whatever do you mean? She is in the san under Matron's eye. She went to her two nights ago with a blinding headache, and we are keeping her under observation to try to find out what the matter is.'

The girls were absolutely taken aback. Sally went brilliant red. She oughtn't to have believed those rumours! But she had wanted to believe them, because she didn't like Ellen. The girls couldn't find a word to say.

Miss Grayling eyed them sharply. 'This is most extraordinary!' she said at last. 'I simply cannot understand it. What made you think Ellen should be expelled? And why did you think she had taken these things? She is surely not that type of girl at all. As you know, she won a scholarship here by means of very hard work and she came with a most excellent report as regards character from her last Head Mistress.'

'We – we thought she had taken them,' began Sally. 'At least, I said we ought not to accuse her till we had definite *proof* – but, but . . .'

'I see. You actually accused the unfortunate girl to her face, I suppose? When was this?'

'The evening before last, Miss Grayling,' said Sally, trying to avoid the Head Mistress's eyes, which had suddenly become gimlets, and were boring into her.

'The evening before last,' said Miss Grayling. 'Ah, that explains matters. It must have been because of that that Ellen got so upset, and was overcome by that fearful headache and went to Matron. And somehow you thought she had been expelled – goodness knows why – some silly rumour, I suppose, fostered by you because you wanted to believe it! You may have done serious damage to an innocent girl.'

Darrell swallowed once or twice. She was remembering how she had attacked Ellen that night in the second-form room. Certainly Ellen had been cheating – but Darrell had called her a thief and said unforgivable things to her. She looked at Miss Grayling and knew that she must tell her what had happened between Ellen and herself. It was because of *that*, she felt sure, that Ellen had been ill that night. Oh dear – how things did begin to go wrong once you were silly yourself!

'Can I say a word to you alone, please, Miss Grayling,' said Darrell, desperately. 'It's something the others don't know about, but I think I'd better tell you.'

'Wait outside the door for a minute or two,' ordered Miss Grayling, nodding at Sally, Belinda and Irene. 'I haven't finished with you yet.'

They went outside and shut the door, feeling surprised. Whatever had Darrell got to tell Miss Grayling? She might at least have told them too!

Darrell poured out the story of how she had followed Ellen that night and caught her in the second-form room cupboard, clutching the test-papers in her hand.

'And I called her a cheat, which she was,' said Darrell, 'and I called her a thief, too, and told her I'd tell Sally in the morning and it would be reported and she would be expelled. And I suppose it worried her so much that she got that awful headache and went to Matron. And I never knew, and we all thought that somehow you must have found out she was a thief and had expelled her quietly, without making a fuss.'

'Well, really!' said Miss Grayling, when this out-pouring had come to an end. 'The things that go on in this school that nobody knows about! It's incredible. Do you actually mean to tell me, Darrell, that you and Ellen were fighting together on the floor of the second-form room in the middle of the night? That is not at all a thing to be proud of.'

'I know,' said Darrell. 'I'm awfully sorry about it now. But I just saw red, Miss Grayling – and lost my temper. I can't bear cheats.'

'It's very strange,' said Miss Grayling, thoughtfully. 'Ellen is a scholarship girl, and I have never known such a girl have any need to cheat. I can't believe that Ellen was cheating. If she was, there is some reason for it that must be found out. Don't any of you like Ellen, Darrell?'

Darrell hesitated. 'Well – she's so nervy and snappy and irritable, Miss Grayling. She snaps if we jerk the table, she shouts at us if we interrupt her reading. She's terribly bad-tempered. I think Jean likes her more than any of us do. She's been awfully patient with her.'

'I wish I'd known all this before,' said Miss Grayling. 'Now I know why Ellen was so upset when I suggested sending her home. I thought possibly she might feel better and happier at home – and she must have thought I was really meaning to expel her, because somebody had come to me and told me she was stealing or cheating. Poor Ellen. I think she has over-taxed that brain of hers and this is the result.'

Darrell stood silent. She felt that Miss Grayling was not very pleased with her. 'I'm sorry for what I did,' she said, trying to blink back the tears. 'I know I keep on and on saying I'll never lose my temper again or lose control of myself. You won't believe me any more.'

'I shall go on believing you and trusting you every single time,' said Miss Grayling, turning her deep-blue eyes on Darrell and smiling. 'And one day you'll be strong enough to keep your promise. Probably when you are in the sixth form! Now tell the others to come in again.'

They came in. Miss Grayling addressed them gravely. 'What Darrell told me I think it is better not to repeat to you for my own good reasons. I think she should not repeat it to you either. I will just say this – Ellen is not the thief, you may be absolutely certain of that.'

'Not the thief!' said Sally. 'But – we all thought she was – and Alicia accused her to her face . . . and . . .'

Sally had let Alicia's name slip without thinking. Miss Grayling drummed on her desk with a pencil. 'Oh – so Alicia did the accusing, did she?' she said. 'Then she has something to feel very guilty about. I think that that public accusation brought Ellen's trouble to a head. Sally, you are head-girl of the form. I leave it to you to show Alicia that a little more kindness and a little less hardness would be very much more admired by me, by you and everyone else.'

'Yes, Miss Grayling,' said Sally, feeling extremely guilty herself. 'But Miss Grayling – who *was* the thief?'

'It couldn't possibly have been Daphne,' said Irene. 'Nobody who did what Daphne did last night could

154

possibly be so mean. Why, Daphne's a heroine! Everyone says so!'

'And you think that if someone does a brave deed quite suddenly, then he or she could never do a mean one?' asked Miss Grayling. 'You are wrong, Irene. We all have good and bad in us, and we have to strive all the time to make the good cancel out the bad. We can never be perfect – we all of us do mean or wrong things at times – but we can at least make amends by trying to cancel out the wrong by doing something worthy later on. Daphne has done quite a bit of cancelling, I think – but her heroic deed doesn't mean that she can never do a small, mean one.'

'Is she the thief then?' asked Sally, incredulously.

'That is what I mean to find out,' said Miss Grayling. 'If she is, she shall tell you herself, and you shall judge her. Now go back to your classroom. I am going to see Daphne in the san. And by the way, Ellen could see someone today. What about Jean? You said she liked Ellen more than any of you did. Tell her to go and see Ellen after tea and be nice to her.'

'Can she tell her we know she's not the thief?' asked Darrell, anxiously. 'And oh, Miss Grayling – could I see her for a few minutes too, by myself?'

'Yes,' said Miss Grayling. 'But no more fighting, Darrell, or Matron will deal very promptly with you indeed!'

21 Daphne, Ellen – and Miss Grayling

Miss Grayling made her way to the san. She spoke to Matron, who nodded. 'Yes, Daphne is quite all right now. She has just got up.'

The Head Mistress told Matron to take Daphne into the next room, where they would be alone. Daphne went, helped along by Matron, and sat down in an arm-chair, wondering rather fearfully what the visit was about. Miss Grayling looked so serious.

'Daphne,' said the Head, 'these things were found in the parcel that Mary-Lou went to post for you. You had packed them up yourself. Where did you get them? And why did you want to send them away?'

She suddenly tipped the purses and the little boxes on to Daphne's knee. The girl stared at them in absolute horror. She went very pale and opened her mouth to speak. But no words came.

'Shall I tell you where you got them from?' said Miss Grayling. 'You took them out of desks and lockers and drawers. You spent the money, Daphne. You did, in fact, exactly what you have done in two other schools, which have quietly intimated to your parents that they would rather have you removed. But they did not tell your parents why.'

'How did you know?' whispered Daphne, her once pretty face white and haggard.

'It is the custom at Malory Towers to get a confidential report of any new girl's character from her previous Head Mistress,' said Miss Grayling. 'We do not, if we can help it, take girls of bad character, Daphne.'

'Why did you take me then?' asked Daphne, not daring to meet the Head's eyes.

'Because, Daphne, your last Head Mistress said that you were not *all* bad,' said Miss Grayling. 'She said that perhaps a fresh start in a fine school like this, with its traditions of service for others, for justice, kindliness and truthfulness, might help you to cancel out the bad and develop the good. And I like to give people a chance.'

'I see,' said Daphne. 'But I'm worse than you think, Miss Grayling. I haven't only stolen – I've told lies. I said I'd never been to another school before, because I was afraid the girls might get to know I'd been sent home twice from schools. I pretended my people were very rich. I – I had a photo on my dressing-table that wasn't my mother at all – it was a very grand picture of a beautiful woman . . .'

'I know,' said Miss Grayling. 'The staff were warned about you, but not the girls. I have heard many things that made me sad, Daphne, made me think that you did not deserve the chance you had been given. Your greatest drawback is your prettiness – you want to make people admire you, you want to make them think you come of handsome, distinguished parents, from a wealthy home – you have to have envy and admiration, don't you? And because your parents are not as grand as you feel they ought to be, with you for a daughter, and cannot afford to give you as much pocket-money and pretty things as the others, you take what you want – you steal.'

'I'm no good,' said Daphne, and she looked down at her hands. 'I know that. I'm just no good.'

'And yet you have done a very brave thing,' said Miss Grayling. 'Look at me, please, Daphne. The girls admire you today – they call you a heroine. They want to cheer you and clap you. You have plenty of good in you!'

Daphne had raised her head and was looking at Miss Grayling. She flushed. 'I'm to blame for what happened to Mary-Lou,' she said. 'When I heard that Ellen had been expelled for stealing the things I had really stolen myself, I was afraid. I was too much of a coward to own up – but I thought if the empty purses and the boxes were found, my finger-prints would be on them and I'd be found out. So I thought I'd send them away by post, to a made-up address. And Mary-Lou knew I was anxious to get the parcel off and that's how she met her accident.'

'I see,' said Miss Grayling. 'I wondered why you sent away the things, Daphne. It is a great mercy that you found Mary-Lou when you did. Otherwise your foolishness and wrong-doing might have caused a great tragedy.'

'I suppose you will be sending me home, Miss Grayling,' said Daphne, after a pause. 'My parents will have to know why. They will guess there is some serious reason. They don't pay my fees you know, they couldn't afford to. My godmother does. If *she* knows about this, she will stop paying for my education; I shall have spoiled my whole life. Am I to be sent away, Miss Grayling?'

'I am going to let the girls decide that,' said Miss Grayling, gravely. 'That is, if you are brave enough to let them, Daphne. I want you to go to the second form and tell them the whole story. Confess everything to them and see what they say.'

'Oh, I can't,' said Daphne, and covered her face with her hands. 'After all I've said – and boasted! I can't!'

'Well, you have the choice,' said Miss Grayling, getting up. 'Either I send you home without any more ado – or you put yourself in the hands of your school fellows. It is a hard thing to do, but if you really want to make amends, you will do it. You have some good in you. Now is your chance to show it, even if it means being braver than you were last night!'

She left Daphne and went in to see Ellen. She sat down by her bed. 'Ellen,' she said, 'Daphne is in great trouble. The others will know soon and I have come to tell you myself. It has been discovered that it was she who took all that money and the jewellery that was missing.'

It took a moment for this to sink into Ellen's mind. Then she sat up. '*Daphne*! But the girls thought it was I who took them! They accused me. They'll never believe it was Daphne.'

'They will,' said Miss Grayling, 'because I rather think Daphne herself is going to tell them! And now, Ellen, tell me – what made you take those test-papers the other night? You are a scholarship girl with brains – you did not need to cheat.'

Ellen lay down again suddenly. She was overcome with shame. How did Miss Grayling know? Had Darrell told everyone then? Of course she had.

'Nobody knows except Darrell and myself,' said Miss Grayling. 'Darrell told me, but told no one else. So you need not worry. But I want to know why you did it. There is something you are worrying about, Ellen, and these headaches of yours won't go until you are at peace with yourself and have lost whatever worry it is you have.'

'I *did* need to cheat,' said Ellen, in a small voice. 'My brain wouldn't work any more. And I got these headaches. I knew I wouldn't even pass the tests – and the girls that night accused me of being a thief, which I wasn't – and I got all hopeless and thought that I might as well be a cheat if they all though I was a thief!'

'I see,' said Miss Grayling. 'But why wouldn't your brain work any more?'

'I don't know,' said Ellen. 'Because I'd worked it a bit too hard, I expect, when I went in for the Scholarship. You see, Miss Grayling, I'm not really very brilliant. I get good results because I slog so – I go on and on, working and studying, where perhaps a real Scholarship girl can get better results with half the work. I worked all through the hols too. I was tired when I got here – but I did so badly want to do well my first term.'

'Did it matter so much?' asked Miss Grayling, gently.

'Yes,' said Ellen. 'I didn't want to let my people down. They've had to pay out more than they can afford really for my uniform and things. They're so proud of me. I *must* do well. And now I've ruined everything.'

'Not quite!' said Miss Grayling, feeling very much relieved to find that simple overwork was at the root of Ellen's trouble, and worry about what her family would think. 'I shall write your parents a letter to tell them that you have worked very hard and done well, but that you are over-strained and must have a real holiday when it comes. By next term you will be quiet fresh again, and you will have forgotten all this and be ready to rush up to the top of the form!'

Ellen smiled at the Head, and the little worried cleft in her forehead disappeared like magic. 'Thank you,' she said gratefully. 'I'd like to say a lot more, but I can't.'

Miss Grayling popped in to have a word with Mary-Lou, and then went back to her own quarters. So many girls – so many problems – so much responsibility in putting things right, and getting the best out of every girl! No wonder Miss Grayling had more grey hairs than she should have had.

22 Daphne owns up. The end of term

Immediately after tea that day the second form were told by Miss Parker that they were to go to their common-room and wait there.

'Why?' asked Belinda, in surprise.

'You'll see,' said Miss Parker. 'Go along now. Some-one is waiting there for you.'

They all went, and rushed pell-mell into the common-room, wondering what the mystery was. Mary-Lou was there, looking a little scared, wrapped in her dressing-gown. Matron had carried her down.

And Daphne was there, fully dressed! The girls rushed at her. 'Daphne! You're a heroine! Daphne! Well done! You saved Mary-Lou's life!'

Daphne did not answer. She sat there and looked at them, rather white in the face, and did not even smile.

'What's the matter?' asked Gwendoline.

'Sit down, all of you,' said Daphne. 'I've got something to say. Then I shall go away and you won't see me again.'

'Good gracious! Why all this melodrama?' asked Jean, disquieted by Daphne's tragic voice.

'Listen,' said Daphne. 'You've got to listen. I'm the thief. I took those things. I've been sent away from two schools already for much the same thing. Miss Grayling knew that, but she wanted to give me another chance. So I came here. I told you lies – especially Gwen. We haven't a yacht. We haven't three or four cars. I told you I'd never been to school before because I didn't want anyone to find out I'd been expelled. I hadn't enough money to pay for some of the subs Jean wanted, and how could I say that, when you all thought my father was a millionaire? So I took money and purses. And I took jewellery too, because I like pretty things and haven't nearly enough myself.'

She paused. The faces round her were shocked and horrified. Gwendoline looked as if she was about to faint. Her grand friend with her millionaire father! No wonder Daphne had never asked her to stay for the holidays. It was all lies.

'You all look shocked. I knew you would be. Miss Grayling said I was to come and confess to you myself, and you would judge me. I can see you judging me now. I don't blame you. I've judged myself, too, and I hate myself! I let you accuse Ellen wrongly, I let you . . .'

'And I fell into the trap and accused Ellen!' said Alicia, in a shamed voice. 'You are a beast, Daphne. You could have stopped me. I shall never forgive myself for doing that to poor old Ellen.'

There was a long pause. Then Sally spoke. 'Is that all, Daphne?'

'Isn't it enough?' said Daphne, bitterly. 'Perhaps you want to know why I got the wind up and sent away those things in a parcel, which poor Mary-Lou took for me. Well, when the rumour went round that Ellen was expelled for thieving, I was scared those purses and things might be discovered, with my finger-prints on. I know the police always look for prints. So I thought I'd better pack them up, put a false address on and send them away through the post. Then nobody would trace them to me. And because of that idiotic idea, Mary-Lou nearly got killed.'

'Yes – and because of that, you came out after me, and risked your own life for me!' said Mary-Lou's soft voice. She got up and went to Daphne. 'I don't care what the others say. I'll stick by you, Daphne. I don't want you to go. You won't ever take things again here now, I know. There's more good in you than bad.'

'Well, I'm sure I don't want to have anything more to do with her,' said Gwendoline, in a disgusted voice. 'If my mother knew . . .'

'Shut up, Gwendoline,' said Darrell. 'I'm sticking by Daphne too. I've done some pretty awful things this week myself, though I can't tell you what. And I think this –

whatever wrong Daphne has done this term is cancelled out completely by her courage last night! We thought her deed was brave and noble then – and what she has just told us now doesn't make it any less brave or noble.'

'I agree with you,' said Sally. 'She's cancelled out her wrong with a right, as far as I'm concerned. And what's more, it wanted courage to come and face us all like this. You've got plenty of that, Daphne. If we stick by you and help you, will it make any difference to you? I mean – will you stop any underhand ways and mean tricks?'

'Do you mean that?' said Daphne, a sudden hope making her face shine. 'What about the others?'

'I'm with Sally and Darrell,' said Jean.

'So am I,' said Belinda, and Irene nodded too. Emily thought for a moment and added her word as well.

'Yes, I'll agree,' she said. 'I think you've behaved terribly badly, Daphne – and terribly well too. At any rate you ought to have a chance to make good.'

'You, Alicia?' said Sally. Alicia had been very silent for the last few minutes. She was overcome with remorse about Ellen. She raised her eyes.

'It seems to me that I need to have a chance given to me to make good, as much as Daphne,' she said, shame-facedly. 'I've been worse than any of you.'

'You have been very hard and merciless, Alicia,' said Sally. 'You jeer at me for wanting to get proof before we accuse people, and for wanting to be fair and kind – but it's better in the end.'

'I know,' said Alicia. 'I do know that. I'm sorry. I've disliked you because you were head-girl instead of me this term, Sally. I've been a perfect idiot. I'm not the one to judge Daphne. I'll follow your lead, you may be sure.'

'Well, it seems as if it's only Gwendoline who is standing out,' said Sally, turning to the sulky-looking girl. 'Poor Gwendoline! She's lost her grand friend and can't get over it. Well, we'll go and tell Miss Grayling that we are all agreed on the matter except Gwendoline. We want to give Daphne another chance, and we don't want her to go.'

'No, don't do that,' said Gwendoline, alarmed at the thought of appearing small and mean to Miss Grayling. 'I agree too.'

'And you agree, Daphne?' said Sally, looking at the quiet girl in the chair.

'Thank you, Sally. With all my heart,' said Daphne, and turned her head away. It was a great moment in her life – the forking of the ways. It was up to her to take the right way and she knew it. If only she was strong enough to!

A timid hand touched her arm. It was Mary-Lou. 'Come back to Matron now,' she said. 'She told us we were to, as soon as the meeting was over. I'll help you up the stairs.'

Daphne smiled for the first time, and this time it was a real smile, a sincere one, not turned on for the sake of being charming. 'You're the one that needs helping up!' she said. 'Come on, or Matron will be hounding us out of here.'

Jean went to see Ellen – a very different Ellen. Things seemed to be clearing up magically. 'I feel miles better now,' said Ellen. 'I'm not doing any more real lessons this term, Jean, and no work at all in the hols. I shan't snap and snarl any more either. I've lost that awful headache that made me so jumpy. It suddenly went after I'd had a talk with Miss Grayling. It was most extraordinary.'

'You're lucky to be in bed just now,' said Jean. 'The tests are simply awful. You should have seen the maths one, Ellen. Honestly I could only do half the sums. But the French one, set by Mam'zelle Dupont, was wizard.'

What with one thing and another, the week of tests passed very quickly and then it was the last week of all. Mistresses began to look harassed as the task of adding up marks, correcting papers, making out reports, grew heavier and heavier. Mam'zelle Dupont worked herself up into a frenzy because she had lost her beautifully added-up marks list, and begged Miss Parker to do it for her again.

Miss Parker wouldn't. 'I've enough worries of my own,' she said. 'You're as bad as Belinda, Mam'zelle. She managed to answer a history test when all the rest of the class were doing a geography paper. Don't ask me how. That girl is the worst scatter-brain I ever saw in my life. How she got hold of a history paper when I had given out geography tests . . .'

'But why didn't she point out the mistake to you?' asked Mam'zelle, astonished.

'She said she didn't even *notice* that the questions were history ones,' groaned Miss Parker. 'These girls! They will be the death of me. Thank goodness there are only two more days till the end of term!'

Only two more days. But what hectic ones! Packing things, looking for things, losing things, exchanging addresses, tidying cupboards, stacking books, cleaning paintpots . . . all the thrilling little things that come at the end of term, and add to the excitement of going home.

'It's been a strange sort of term,' said Darrell to Sally. 'Don't you think so, Sally? I'm not very pleased with some of the things I've done. You've been fine, though. You always are.'

'Rubbish!' said Sally. 'You don't know how many times I've hated Alicia for defying me. You don't know lots of things about me!'

'I've enjoyed this term though,' said Darrell, remembering everything. 'It's been interesting. Ellen and her snappiness – and the way we all thought wrong things about her – and now it's all come right and she's quite different and she and Jean are as thick as thieves together!'

'And then Daphne,' said Sally, the word 'thieves' bringing her to mind. 'That was an extraordinary affair, wasn't it, Darrell? I'm glad we gave her a chance. Isn't it funny the way she's dropped that silly Gwendoline Mary and taken Mary-Lou for her friend?'

'Jolly good thing,' said Darrell. 'Mary-Lou may be a timid little thing – but she's sound at heart. And it's much better for her to have a friend of her own than go tagging after us all the time. But I shall always like little Mary-Lou.'

'Gwendoline looks sour these days,' said Sally, nudging her friend as Gwendoline went by alone. 'Nobody's darling now!'

'Won't do her any harm,' said Darrell, hard-heartedly. 'She'll soon be Mother's darling and Miss Winter's darling, and have her bed made for her and everything done! Dear darling Gwendoline Mary. She didn't come very well out of the Daphne affair, did she?'

'No, she didn't. Perhaps she'll be better next term,' said Sally, doubtfully. 'Oh, my goodness, what *is* Belinda doing?'

Belinda shot by with a work-basket in her arms, from which trailed yards and yards of wool and cotton. It wound itself round people's ankles and legs and at last forced her to stop.

'Get off my cottons!' she yelled indignantly. 'You're holding me up!'

'Oh, Belinda – you'll always be an idiot!' cried Darrell, unwinding some red wool from her right ankle. 'Go away! I'm getting a forest of cotton round me. Belinda, don't forget to bring back a whole lot of funny sketches after the hols.'

'I will!' said Belinda, with a grin. 'And what about Alicia thinking up a new trick for next term. Hi, Alicia, we've thought of some holiday prep for you! Make up some super tricks for next term, see?'

'Right!' called Alicia. 'I will. You can bank on that! Better than the "OY!" on Mam'zelle's back, Darrell!'

'Oy! What is an Oy?' demanded Mam'zelle Dupont, bustling up. 'An "OY!" on my back? What is this you have done to me now?'

She screwed herself round, trying to see what an 'OY' was, and the girls screamed with laughter.

'It's all right, Mam'zelle. It's not there now.'

'But what *is* an "OY"?' demanded Mam'zelle. 'I shall ask Miss Parker.'

But Miss Parker was not interested in Mam'zelle's 'OY's. She was only interested in getting the girls safely away on holiday. Then she could sit down and breathe in peace.

And at last they were really off. Cars swung into the drive. The train-girls went off singing. Belinda rushed frantically back for her suitcase, which she had as usual forgotten.

'Good-bye, Malory Towers!' yelled the girls. 'Good-bye, Potty! Good-bye, Nosey! Good-bye, Mam'zelle Oy!'

'They're gone,' said Mam'zelle. 'Ah, the dear, dear girls, how I love to see them come – and how I love to see them go! Miss Parker, you must tell me, please. What is this "Oy"? I have never heard of it.'

'Look it up in the dictionary,' said Miss Parker, as if she was speaking to her class. 'Four weeks of peace, blessed peace. I can't believe it!'

'They will soon be back, these bad girls,' said Mam'zelle. And she was right. They will!